Love Between the Vines

Romancing the Dog series

Love Between the Vines

Romancing the Dog series

One of three romance novellas
by
Marjorie Pinkerton Miller

SUNACUMEN
PRESS
Colorado Springs, CO

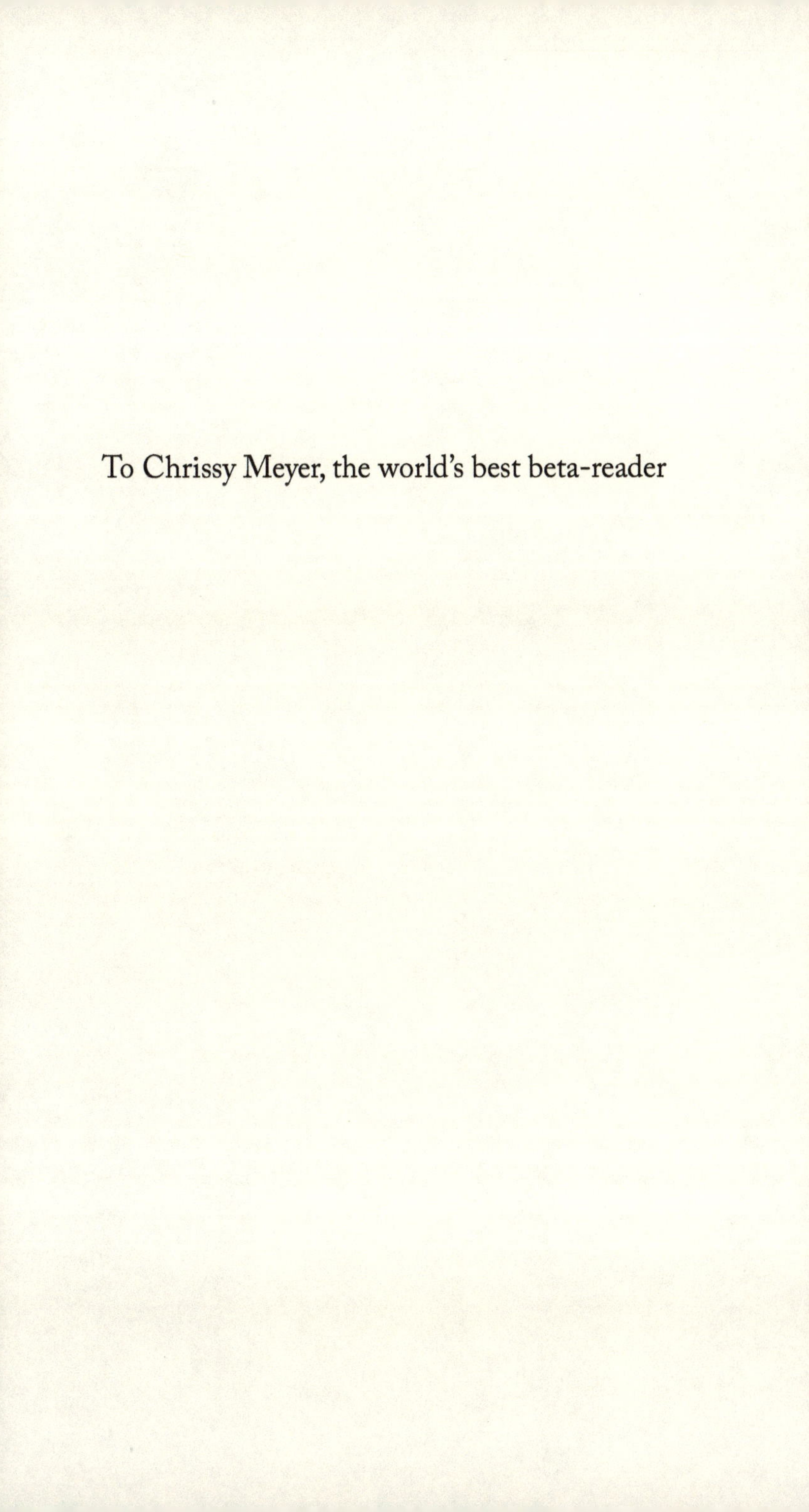

To Chrissy Meyer, the world's best beta-reader

One

THE HOST INSIDE THE RESTAURANT entrance greeted Thomas like an old friend.

"Your regular table, Thomas?"

Sofia was surprised. Regular table?

"Thanks, Tyler," said Thomas. "That will be fine."

"How often do you come here?" Sofia asked quietly as she stepped around the host stand to follow Tyler into the hushed bowels of the restaurant.

"About once a week," Thomas whispered.

Tyler led them through the labyrinth of tables, past well-dressed and coifed patrons, to a table for two in a dark corner at the back of the restaurant. No one looked up as they passed.

The host pulled out a chair for Sofia and bent slightly toward her. "I don't believe we've met."

Although he didn't extend a hand to shake, Sofia took the cue and introduced herself. "Sofia Michaelis."

"Well, any friend of Thomas's is a friend of mine." He nodded, smiled politely, and handed Thomas the wine list.

"Actually, I'm his fiancée," Sofia said.

The host paused a beat.

"Of course," he responded with an apologetic glance toward Thomas. "I should have remembered." He handed Thomas a large, heavy leather menu.

Thomas opened what Sofia assumed was the wine list. "Could you send the sommelier?" he asked without looking up at either of them.

"Immediately." The host retreated.

"You're here once a week?" Sofia continued to pursue her question.

"We have most our business lunches here," Thomas explained, keeping his voice low. "We have an account."

"Why didn't I know this?"

Thomas flashed his patronizing, crooked smile—one that he had only recently begun using whenever he didn't want to discuss something she wanted to talk about.

"It's not important," he said, his voice as condescending as his smile.

"So, you have business meetings back here at a table for two once a week?" Sofia asked as soon as the host was out of earshot. "It seems a bit cozy. What if there are three of you?"

Thomas studied the wine list, ignoring her question. Sofia stared at him, but he refused to take her bait. Lately, he'd left a lot of questions unanswered, and she had come to feel there was a lot she didn't understand about Thomas's advertising firm.

As her eyes adjusted to the dark interior, Sofia glanced around. In the corner, a pianist touched his keys so lightly it took her a moment to identify the song he was playing over the clink of forks on china and hushed conversations. The crowd little resembled the patrons she was accustomed to dining with here in Seattle. Most of the men wore suits, even though ties and top buttons had been loosened to accommodate the evening. The women's suits and dresses were not ones Sofia had seen on the sale racks at Nordstrom, where she shopped. Designer, she guessed.

Thomas wore his usual Seattle business attire—khaki pants and a blue blazer, no tie. His thick thatch of blond hair masked his age, but Sofia had noticed over the past six months how all those business lunches had softened his once-trim physique.

She wore her best dress—a red knit with a pinched waist that showed off her slim figure. But it was modest compared with the fine couture that surrounded them. She fingered the modest diamond pendant at her nick. It was certainly the least expensive piece of jewelry in the room.

The sudden, silent approach of the sommelier surprised her. Thomas looked up.

"We'll have a bottle of Dom Perignon, 1990." The man nodded appreciatively and turned away.

"That's really not necessary, Thomas," Sofia said. "We can drink all the free bubbly we want next week when we're on vacation."

"Yes, I know." Thomas shook his head. "But that would be Walla Walla bubbly. I wanted this anniversary dinner to be special."

"It's already special," she said. "You know this is the first relationship I've ever had that lasted three years?"

Thomas continued to stare at the wine menu. Sofia reached across the table and put her hand on his.

"I'm really looking forward to getting away next week, aren't you?" she said. "It's the first time I think we've ever had my parents' place to ourselves."

A waiter slid up and gently laid dinner menus in front of them, making Sofia jump. The extremely muted nature of the room was getting on her nerves. Was she going to cringe each time someone approached their table? This kind of fine dining wasn't in her budget, and she realized she was glad it wasn't.

Thomas laid the wine menu down and picked up the dinner menu, still without meeting her eye. "Can we order first? I am famished."

Resigned to his cold shoulder, Sofia picked up her menu. "What do you think you'll have?"

AN HOUR LATER, THEIR PLATES clean, Sofia sat back with her last half of a glass of red wine. She had ordered the sockeye salmon and would have preferred a white wine with dinner, but Thomas ordered a cabernet without consulting her.

It hadn't been much of an anniversary dinner, in Sofia's estimation. Thomas had grunted out a few responses to her questions about his work and his progress toward getting the promotion he wanted, but he'd asked her nothing. It seemed odd. He used to have plenty of advice for her about the marketing she managed for a local microbrewery. Since they both worked in marketing, they once had much to talk about and share. Over time, though, he'd withdrawn, and at first, Sofia had chalked it up to the stress over work. But lately when they did talk about work, he shrewdly intimated his were the loftier concerns of a marketing executive, not a low-level practitioner.

Thomas caught the attention of their waiter and crooked his finger at him. The waiter hurried over.

"Can we have the check, please?" he asked. It was the first "please" Sofia had heard him utter all night.

"Can't we sit here for a few minutes?" she protested. "I still have quite a bit of wine left." Sofia picked up her glass and swirled the liquid to demonstrate.

"I'm sorry. I just remembered I have an early meeting tomorrow," he said with a forced smile.

"With your new marketing director?"

"What? Why would you ask that?"

Thomas pressed his eyebrows together.

"Well, you've just been working with her a lot lately. I guess it's a lot of work to break in a new employee."

"Well, yes, it is. But what was that inuendo?"

Sofia had intended none, but she tilted her head apologetically.

"I'm sorry. I didn't mean to suggest anything. I know it's crazy at work for you right now. I know you want that promotion. It will be nice to be away—"

Thomas interrupted. "About that. I am not sure I can make it after all."

Sofia put her glass down hard; the wine came close to sloshing over the edge. "What do you mean? We've been planning this trip for two months!"

Thomas grimaced. "I know. And I was really looking forward to it. But we have this new marketing team in Denver, and I have to go out there and get them started. It's only for a few days."

"But—"

"You know how important work is to me. I'm working my butt off to get that promotion. If I get this team off to a good start, I have a good chance at executive VP."

Sofia pouted. "But this is important for us, too. We haven't been away from work forever. We haven't gone out of town together since last May. That was more than a year ago!"

"I know." Thomas reached over and placed his hand on hers. "I'll make it up to you, I promise. But you should go anyway. You need some vineyard time. I know how much you love the wine country. It's in your blood. And you can spend some time touching up your golf game."

He pulled his hand away and reached in his jacket pocket for his wallet. "Besides, you promised your parents you'd take care of Rufus while they're on vacation. And

Rufus isn't very fond of me. Go without me."

Sofia looked away, blinking at the sting of tears. The waiter arrived and lay the leather American Express portfolio next to Thomas's hand. Thomas put his credit card on top of it and handed it back.

"Let's split this," Sofia said, pulling her purse off the back of her chair.

"No, I insist," he said. "It's my anniversary present. And it's not often I have the chance to dine with the prettiest girl in Seattle."

"It would be a lot more often if you gave me the time." Sofia forced a smile, but she couldn't alter the bitterness in her voice. She knew she was pretty—always had been. His compliment meant little to her, and she guessed it meant little to him as well.

Thomas met her eyes. "I know, but really, Sofia, you should go to Walla Walla. You've been working so hard, and you deserve this time off. Go."

Sofia looked away again and considered. "Maybe I will. But you'll call me from Denver, okay? That will make it seem like you're with me. A little."

Two

Sofia held her phone on her shoulder with a tilt of her head while she pulled the packaging off a frozen dinner. Diet, of course, but not cheap.

"Yes, Mom," she said into the phone. "I know. But he has to go to Denver for a meeting with the new marketing team there. Otherwise, I'm sure he'd come with me."

She could envision her mother in her kitchen in Walla Walla, her bobbed hair held perfect with just the right amount of spray, her make-up expertly applied even though only Sofia's father was likely to see her all day.

"Honey, I hate to remind you. But this is what happened when you planned to go to Palm Springs last year," her mother said. "Does he ever follow through? Does he ever commit to anything? And speaking of commitment, when is he going to put that ring on your finger?"

"Mother, I'm not in as much of a hurry for a ring as you are," Sofia answered. "And I'm not sure it would change his behavior. He's all about work right now. That promotion he wants, you know."

"Well, perhaps you shouldn't marry him, anyway."

Sofia rolled her eyes and opened the microwave, nearly losing the phone off her shoulder. She caught it, stuck it back under her ear, and punched in the frozen dinner settings. The microwave started to whir.

"I don't know what you're saying, Mom. One minute you ask when we're getting married and the next you say maybe we shouldn't. I know you've ever really liked Thomas. Maybe if you spent more time—"

Her mother interrupted. "I don't know how we can spend more time with him when he doesn't even have time for you. He has refused to come back here since that first year you were dating. I think he doesn't care for us."

"I think it's probably more that he doesn't care for Walla Walla. He keeps telling me he's a big city guy. I expect at some point he will have his eye on a job in New York City."

Sofia set out a plate and fork on the kitchen bar and pulled a sheet off the roll of paper towels for a napkin while she listened to her mother describe her only trip to the Big Apple a year ago. Sofia had heard it a dozen times. "I have never been so happy to see the Walla Walla wheat fields in my life as I was when we got back," her mother concluded.

"I know, Mom. I've heard it before."

The microwave dinged.

"Is that the microwave?" her mother asked. "Are you eating that junk food again?"

"It's not junk food, Mom. It's a high-end frozen dinner."

"Oxymoron if I've ever heard one," her mother quipped.

Sofia laughed, switched her phone to speaker mode, and set down the plastic dish. She pulled off the hot plastic wrap and tossed it in the sink.

"So, I guess I'm going to come anyway," she said before

she sat down to eat. "I want to see Rufus and chill for a while. I might even bring my golf clubs."

"Oh, honey, you should. The courses here are in the best shape I've seen in years."

"And you and Dad have a great time in Sun Valley. I know how much you love it there in the summer. That's where I met Thomas, remember?"

"Yes, I do remember," her mother answered. "Oh, one minor complication. Your brother arranged to have a friend of his stay at our house for a couple of weeks to study winery marketing. He'll get here on Friday, the day after you come."

"What? Who is it? Do I know this guy?"

"His name is Enzo, and he met your brother in Mendoza a couple of months ago. He is going to visit some tasting rooms and talk with some wineries about how to do wine tours. I guess his family owns a winery. It's hard to believe, but your brother says that Walla Walla is ahead of Argentina when it comes to wine tourism."

Sofia put her fork down, cancelled speaker mode, and put the phone back to her ear. "But Mom! I don't know this guy! How can I share the house with him? What if he's a creep?"

"Michael says he's a really great guy. And this is a very large house, Sofia. You know that. You grew up here. We'll put him in the west wing. You can have your old room. You won't even see him much. And if you want to set some house rules, go ahead."

Sofia shook her head. First Thomas cancelled on her, and now this. "Maybe I should come another time," she said. "This guy ... what's his name?"

"Enzo."

"Wow, how exotic," Sofia said as sarcastically as she could. "Enzo. Maybe he can take care of Rufus for you. I'll come another time."

"No one can take care of Rufus like you, Sofia. I think you should still come. Rufus misses you."

It didn't take much imagination for Sofia to see her mother bend down to scratch Rufus's ears as she cooed, "He's such a good boy!"

"You're not trying to set me up with some stranger because you don't like Thomas, are you, Mother?" Sofia put the phone back on speaker and took a bite of chicken.

"Of course not. I had nothing to do with inviting this young man. I've never met him. We're just helping a friend of Michael's. You know how much it costs to stay in a hotel for two weeks."

Sofia choked and grabbed her water to clear her throat. "Two full weeks? Are you serious? So, he'll be there the entire time I'm there?"

"Sofia! This is not about you. Come on, I'd think you'd be happy to have company now that Thomas isn't coming. I understand he plays a little golf. Maybe you two—"

"Mother! I am not playing golf with him or entertaining him or taking him around town. Nothing. Okay? This is my vacation. I need some peace and quiet. I want to come, but I need him to leave me alone."

"Just tell him that, dear. I'm sure he speaks fine English."

Sofia wasn't going to win this argument. "Okay. I'll be there Thursday. But I am in no mood to put up with some Latin playboy. I hope he's on his best behavior. Remember Julio? He was from Argentina, too."

Her mother laughed. "Yes, I remember Julio, dear. But that was a long, long time ago. And you're the one who's always telling me not to judge someone by where they come from."

Three

Nothing in the Walla Walla airport had changed that Sofia could see, but it bustled with summer tourists. It had been a year since she'd been home—the May before last when she and Thomas cancelled their vacation to Palm Springs, and she took a solo trip back to the vineyards instead.

She waited in line at the rental car agency, collected her rollerbag and her golf clubs from the baggage carousels, and stepped outside into the bright sunshine. The sun hurt her eyes. It was July, but it was still raining in Seattle, and she wasn't used to the bright light. She took a deep breath of dry air, pulled her sunglasses down from the top of her head, and headed for the car lot.

The wine tasting rooms in the business park just east of the airport tempted her, but Sofia looked at her watch and decided noon was too early to start drinking. And it was better to let someone else drive if she decided to visit some of her favorite wineries. Anyway, she wanted to be sure to get settled in the house and establish her territory before Enzo showed up.

Instead of turning onto the highway to head directly to her parents' house west of town, though, she drove the three miles to downtown. Already, wine tourists were sauntering down the street and filling the sidewalk cafés. Sofia remembered when Walla Walla was still a sleepy farm town, and it was more common to see tractors and combines on main street than Lexus's and Mercedes. Wine had transformed her hometown during her junior high and high school years, and it appeared the transformation wasn't slowing down.

Sofia drove slowly, turning her head from side to side, noting the new tasting rooms and bistros that had sprung up in just the past year. Her curiosity sated, she turned north on Second Avenue, glancing at the Maison Bleue Winery storefront, happy to see it was still in business. She'd spent many afternoons in high school working in store room, helping with shipping. She pulled onto the highway and headed west, passing the Wine Valley Golf Club sign before turning off and winding her way around, over the creek, and finally up a steep hill to home.

From the top of the driveway, rows of grapevines ran down the hill where apple orchards once dominated the landscape. Sofia sat in the car for a minute, taking in the familiar sights. Far down below, the Waterbrook Winery's pond shone in the mid-day sun.

She rolled down the window and took a deep breath. The hot dry earth smelled like home. How long, she wondered, would she have to be gone before coming back here felt unfamiliar, like some distant past?

Shaking herself out of her reverie, she picked up her purse and headed up the path to the stately house her parents had built atop their vineyards more than a dozen years ago. Ten years later, they retired from viticulture and sold the vineyards, but they'd held onto the big house, unable to part with the quiet of the countryside and the views.

Out of the corner of her eye, Sofia spotted a big, furry mass bouncing toward her. She dropped her purse and leaned down to give Rufus the welcome he expected. Rufus rammed his big head into her knees, nearly knocking her off her feet.

Laughing and scratching his ears, Sofia gave the Bernese Mountain Dog a big hug and let his big tongue lap her face before she pushed him away. She picked up her purse, headed toward the front door, and pulled the house key from her bag. She turned it in the slot, but the door wasn't locked. Had her parents left the house open? That certainly didn't seem like something her father would do. Suddenly, the door flew open and Sofia was nearly run over by a tall, dark-haired man.

Sofia screamed and fell back, tripping over Rufus. The man reached out and caught her by the elbow before she hit the ground.

Regaining her balance, Sofia glanced up at a tanned, handsome face framed by a surfeit of thick, dark hair. His dark eyes danced with amusement.

"You must be Enzo," she said, shaking loose of his hand and sticking hers out for a shake. "At least I hope you are. I thought you were coming tomorrow."

The stranger ignored her hand, grabbed her shoulders, and leaned in to kiss her on both cheeks. Rufus bounced excitedly between them, forcing them apart.

"Yes, I am Enzo. And you must be the lovely Sofia." The first words out of Enzo's mouth sounded so familiar, and Sofia was transported back to the summer before her senior year in high school when Julio was staying with her family. His accent was exactly the same.

Enzo backed up and looked Sofia up and down, finally

settling his eyes on hers. "And you are much better looking than your brother said."

Sofia felt herself blush and tried to cover it with a frown. Somehow when Thomas said things like that these days, it didn't affect her. But Enzo's compliment certainly did.

"You got here early," she said. Her throat was tight, and Sofia forced her voice to drop pitch. "I thought you weren't coming until tomorrow."

"I guess Michael had my arrival wrong," Enzo said. His English was perfect, but his accent continued to give Sofia flashbacks. "I met your parents, though. They are very nice people."

Sofia paused for a moment to get her bearings. She wasn't going to allow this man to change her plans for the week, as she had told her mother. She needed to get over his appearance and his sexy accent right away, or things could go astray in a very bad way. She straightened up and threw her shoulders back.

"Okay," she said in as bossy a tone as she could muster. "So you're here. I want to get something straight right away."

Enzo backed away, his eyebrows raised, and Sofia continued. "I need some R and R, and I'm not here to entertain anyone but Rufus. I don't cook or clean for anyone but myself, and I expect you to respect my parents' home and give me space."

A smile started to creep across Enzo's face until he forced it to stop.

"I came here to be alone and to see some old friends," Sofia said. "I would appreciate it if you make yourself as scarce as you can."

Enzo frowned, and Sofia imagined he was accustomed to a much different reaction from women he met. Probably. With those dark eyes and slim figure, he most likely got nothing but swoons in his presence.

"Ooookay, boss woman!" He backed up another step and pushed the front door open. "You are as tough as your brother said you were."

Sofia bent down to pick up her purse. "What does that mean?"

"Oh, don't get me wrong," Enzo said, taking a little bow. "I love tough women. I promise I will stay out of your way. I promise. Don't want to get in trouble with the boss."

Sofia rolled her eyes and headed back to the car to get her bag out of the trunk. Enzo followed, and as she popped open the trunk, he reached in for her bag. "Let me get that," he said.

Sofia slapped his arm away. "No! Really! Don't you understand English? I asked you to give me space!"

Enzo backed up, his hands in the air.

"Whoa!" he exclaimed. "Bad flight?"

Sofia slammed the trunk shut and lugged her rollerbag clumsily up the uneven path, Rufus at her heels. She felt Enzo's eyes on her back and heard him mutter, "Wow, Michael didn't prepare me for this."

Four

OF THE THIRTY-PLUS TASTING ROOMS now dotting Walla Walla's Main Street and a couple blocks of side streets, Sofia had her favorites, and she was pleased to see they hadn't changed much in a year. A couple that she'd never been fond of had disappeared, replaced by new labels that Sofia hoped to try before she headed back to Seattle the next week.

The room Sofia and Janet chose to visit her first afternoon in town was quiet for a Thursday, which worried Sofia. Quiet was good after noisy Seattle, but it could mean the bloom was off this particular winery's rosé, and it too would be replaced by a shiny newcomer soon.

As they relaxed on the tasting room sofa with full glasses of a pleasantly dry viognier, Sofia looked her best friend over with a critical eye. She'd always been afraid of staying in a small town like Walla Walla, where youthful fashion sense and fitness would be replaced by grown-up complacency, but from what she saw in Janet, she had been worried for no reason. Janet's soft blonde curls were as well tended as her petite frame, and her work clothes were quite a few levels above what Sofia wore to work at the brewery in Seattle every day.

Janet appeared to be making the same assessment, and her evaluation of Sofia wasn't as benign.

"I have to say, you've looked better, Sofia," she said frowning.

Sofia laughed uncomfortably. "Gee, thanks. With friends like you ... ."

"No, I'm serious. You look tired and stressed."

"Well, that's why I'm here!" Sofia's gesture was a little too emphatic, and she sloshed a little wine onto the couch. She wiped at it, and it rolled right off. Tasting room upholstery, of course, was chosen for its impermeability.

"I know I need a little R&R," Sofia said, trying not to whine. "But I didn't come to get scolded."

She picked an olive off the plate on the low table in front of them and chewed pensively.

"It is hard, though," she explained. "The brewery is struggling. The new hard cider isn't taking off like it should. Last year, it would have flown off the shelves. Just when we got it perfected and started marketing, everyone suddenly wants hard seltzer."

"I guess it's a good thing you didn't invest in it, then, right?"

Sofia nodded. Janet was a loan officer at the biggest local bank, and she knew finance and investments. Sofia had called her when she was offered an opportunity to buy some shares in the closely held company that owned the brewery.

"Yes, absolutely. You steered me right on that. I really appreciate it. But if the brewery goes under, I'm not going to have a job. That's just about as bad. You know how hard it is to find jobs right now."

Janet took her turn at the appetizer plate and finished a couple of olives before answering.

"You can always come back to Walla Walla," she said finally. "This place is still growing. You know we got two more tasting rooms downtown last year? The town's becoming an international destination."

Sofia was proud of what her hometown had turned into, but she raised an eyebrow at her friend's assertion.

Janet waved her arms at the scene out the big picture window to the street. "Wine tours, bike tours, balloon festivals. You name it. The Whitman Hotel is booked solid all the time, not just in summer like it used to be. They're building a couple new motels on the highway and there'd be more going up if the county would allow it. I just hope we don't get too big. I don't want this place to turn into Denver or something."

Sofia chucked at Janet's enthusiasm. "I don't think you have to worry about that. Speaking of Denver, I guess you see Thomas didn't come."

"Oh, my gosh. I'm sorry. I didn't even ask. Why not? You two haven't broken up, have you?"

"No, although I think we may be the only two people in the world who think we shouldn't. My parents have still not warmed to him."

Janet nodded. "But has he given them a chance? When was the last time he was here?"

"Three years ago. I think." Sofia tried to remember. "We only stayed a day. He had some emergency that meant he had to get back to work. This time, he had to go to Denver for a meeting."

The news appeared to please Janet. "So that means, it's girl time!" she exclaimed. "What do you want to do? We have a bunch of new wines to taste, so of course we'll do that."

"Of course," Sofia smiled. It was great to be back in

a place where people enjoyed and appreciated good wine. "But I'd like to play a little golf too. It's so hard to play in Seattle. I don't like that country club that Thomas belongs to. So hoity-toity. I'd swear they'd all swing their drivers with their pinkies out if they could."

She demonstrated as well as she could without a club in her hand.

"That's not a problem at Wine Valley." Janet laughed. "And I won't make you go to our country club, although it's certainly not snooty. We can play plenty of golf without it."

"And I want to sit up there at home on the hill and look at the vineyard," Sofia continued. "I miss it so much! I love how quiet it is up there. You should come up and stay a couple of nights."

"I'd love to—"

"Oh, but I have to warn you. My brother invited some friend of his to stay up there for the next two weeks." Sofia scrunched up her nose. "Enzo. Quite the charmer," she said mocking his accent. "Or so he thinks."

"But isn't your brother still in Argentina?"

"Yes. And that is where Enzo is from. Came to learn all about wine tourism, I guess. Judging from my last experience with an Argentinian, he's probably looking for other things, too."

Janet picked a slice of cheese off the plate and waved it at Sofia. "You can't judge every Latino by what Julio did to you," she said. "He was just immature. I'm sure there are Argentinians who are out for something other than … ." She stopped.

"Yeah. You remember what Julio wanted," Sofia said. "All he wanted."

"Sofia, you were in high school. Haven't you gotten past that?" Janet finally quit waving the cheese and stuck it in her mouth.

"I would if everyone else would. Every time I come to

town, I feel like everyone is looking at me like 'Isn't that the girl who—"

Janet interrupted. "Oh, that's silly. You need to get over it."

Sofia shook her head and reached for a slice of sausage. "I hope you're right. Anyway, why don't you come up for a glass of wine and a light dinner tonight? I haven't had a chance to cook anything but frozen dinners in ages. You can stay overnight if you want."

Janet considered the offer for a moment before accepting with an upturned thumb. "Okay, I'll bring a toothbrush in case, but if I don't drink too much I'll probably come back down. I have to work tomorrow." Her face brightened. "And I'll get to meet Enzo, right?"

"I don't know. I asked him to give me space. I don't want to cook, clean or entertain for him. But Rufus will be there. I know he misses you as much as he misses me."

Five

THE SUN WAS SHINING BRIGHTLY again the next afternoon when Sofia arrived at the Wine Valley Golf Club. She walked into the pro shop and stood just inside the door to let her eyes adjust to the relatively dim light.

"Hey! It's Sofia!" John, the golf pro, shouted. "Sofia Michaelis! A sight for sore eyes. Haven't seen you in ages."

As her pupils got used to the room, Sofia noted that tall, athletic John looked exactly like she remembered, big smile and all. He was the kind of guy who made friends of everyone who came through the door. At times, Sofia had been jealous of his gregarious energy.

"Hi, John," Sofia walked up to his counter. "Good to see you too."

"How's that beautiful swing of yours?"

"I'm afraid it's not what it used to be. It's a lot harder to get out to play in Seattle. It's not just the rain. It's work. It's the courses. There's nothing there like Wine Valley."

Sofia pulled her billfold out of her purse and handed her credit card across the counter. John put up his hand to stop her.

"Nope. Your money's no good here," he said. "It's on me today."

"Gee, thanks, John." Sofia stuck the card back in its slot.

"Just this once. Don't get used to it. So, you're back in town for good?"

Sofia shook her head. "No, just in and out."

John printed out a ticket and handed it to Sofia along with the keys for a golf cart. "Why don't you move back?" he asked. "If the golf's not so good in the big city, what keeps you there?"

"A job. Ever since Mom and Dad sold the vineyards, there really isn't anything for me to do here."

"Oh, I don't know. Seems like things are booming. Just ask Janet." He gestured at the door to indicate her friend's arrival.

"Hey, sorry I'm late," Janet said.

Sophie greeted her with a quick hug. "No problem. Our tee-time isn't for a half hour. You're not late."

As Janet paid for her round—no freebies for the locals, Sofia noted—Sofia rummaged through the racks of golf clothes, looking for something on sale. It had been ages since she'd had an excuse to buy anything new for golf.

"Come on," Janet called out. "Let's go hit some balls. My guess is you're kind of rusty."

SOFIA'S SWING WAS A LITTLE sluggish, but the driving range faced northeast and a nice breeze from the southwest helped the balls fly farther. A right-handed player, Sofia faced lefty Janet as they worked through their irons and hybrid clubs and finally pulled out their drivers.

The repetitions helped Sofia work out the kinks, and by the time she set a ball on a tee and took a couple of practice swings with her driver, she felt more confident. Each time she stepped up to the ball, she reminded herself what she needed to do. Keep the head behind the ball. Keep the left arm straight, turn the shoulders, start the swing with the hips.

In a second and a half, she saw she hadn't lost all of her game in the six months since she'd last swung a club.

"Nice shot," Janet said, watching Sofia's ball soar out past the two-hundred-yard marker. "It doesn't take you long to get it back."

"I'm kind of surprised." Sofia stopped and watched Janet's drive. Her swing was smooth, but she'd never had Sofia's distance. The ball, nevertheless, caught the wind and came up just short of Sofia's.

Janet let her driver rest and watched Sofia take another shot. "That was fun last night," she said. "It was wonderful to be back up there on that hill, away from traffic and sirens."

Sofia watched her ball land before reaching down to place another one on the tee.

"Ha!" she said, while taking another practice swing. "You should live in Seattle! Walla Walla is as quiet as a funeral parlor compared with that. I'm glad Mr. Obnoxious stayed out of our hair."

"I, for one, was a little disappointed. I wanted to meet Enzo."

Sofia swung again. This time she ignored the ball flight and shook her head at her friend. "Janet! You are happily married. Why would you want to meet him?"

"Just curious. Let me tell you, Sofia, you never stop looking. Even when you don't have to. Even when you're not interested."

Sofia looked over Janet's head up the slight slope behind them and frowned. "Well, then, I guess it's your lucky day. Here he comes."

Janet spun around to watch Enzo walk toward them, a driver and a sack of practice balls in his hands. Enzo waved the club at them. He looked much happier to see them than Sofia was to see him.

"Well, hello, landlady. Fancy meeting you here!"

"Yeah, fancy that," Sofia snarled. "I can't imagine this is some coincidence, is it?"

Enzo ignored Sofia and walked up to Janet. "And who is this gorgeous companion of yours?"

Sofia threw Janet an I-told-you-so look, but Janet's eyes were focused on Enzo.

"This is Janet," Sofia answered. "A friend from high school. A *married* friend."

Enzo glanced at Sofia and smirked. "I certainly hope so," he said. "I'd hate to think all American men are blind to such beauty. *Mucho gusto*, Janet. I'm Enzo."

He leaned in and kissed Janet on both cheeks, drawing a big smile from her.

Sofia rolled her eyes, but neither Enzo nor Janet was looking. She lined up for another shot off the tee, but she gripped the club too tight and topped the ball. It skittered off the tee and bounced about 40 yards in front of them.

Disgusted, Sofia bent down and picked up her tee. "I'm done here, Janet. Let's go see if John will let get out on the course a little early."

Enzo gestured to where her shot had traveled. "Are you sure?" He laughed. "Looks like you could use a little more warm-up."

"Thanks for your evaluation, *señor*," she said, her voice squeaking with sarcasm. "But I don't think I need your advice on the golf course." She slammed her driver back in her bag. "You may know wine, but I know golf."

Sofia pulled the heavy bag onto her shoulder and started up the hill to their golf cart. She turned to watch Janet shrug and trade smiles with Enzo.

"Are you coming or are you just going to stand there making eyes at him?" Sofia hooked her bag on the back of the cart and waited for Janet to catch up. As Janet climbed the hill with her bag, Sofia watched Enzo set a ball on a tee and, without so much of a stretch or a practice swing, send it sailing out onto the range. She didn't wait to see how far it went.

"I'm sorry," John said, scrolling through the tee times booked on the computer in the golf shop. He looked up at Sofia. "You'll have to wait. Your tee-time is only 15 minutes away, and there's a group on the tee right now."

Sofia groaned.

"And," John said, "I hope you don't mind, but we're too busy for twosomes today. I had to pair you with a single. It shouldn't slow you down since there's a foursome out ahead of you anyway."

Sofia made a face and turned to Janet. "I just hope we're not paired with you-know-who."

A minute later, they stood next to the first tee, swinging their drivers to keep their muscles warm.

"You didn't tell me this Enzo was so attractive," Janet said.

"Oh, is he? I didn't notice. He looks exactly like I expected he would. Argentinian."

"Well, I thought you weren't very nice. He is a house guest."

"I didn't invite him. I wanted some peace and quiet. And I don't really care what he looks like."

Janet nodded at the cart coming down the path toward them. "That's good because here he comes. At least he won't distract *you* on the tee."

Sofia swiveled to see Enzo driving up to them in his cart. She slumped like her day had just been spoiled and turned to stare down the first fairway. She took a deep breath and muttered to herself, "I'm not going to let him ruin my first round in six months."

Enzo jumped out of his cart and bounced up toward them, driver and ball in hand. "Well, we meet again! I guess I'm paired up with you two today. Aren't we lucky?"

Sofia turned to face him. "Lucky is not exactly the word I'd use. But fine. I just hope you can keep up with us. I was the captain of the high school golf team, and Janet here was my deputy. We've played this course more times than you have shaved, is my guess."

Enzo grinned and stroked his chin, which, Sofia admitted to herself, looked like it required at least daily shaves.

"I'm intrigued by your confidence, my dear landlady," he said. "I hope I will not hold you back. What tees would you like to play today? Ladies' tees?"

"We don't call them ladies' tees," Sofia snapped. "They're forward tees. And we'll play whatever tees you choose. Are the 'men's tees' okay with you? The whites?"

"Sure. If that works for you." Enzo pointed down the fairway to indicate the group ahead was out of their way. "Go ahead and tee off first. *Ladies.*"

Janet walked up to the tee box. She set her tee and ball in the ground, took a practice swing and hit her tee shot. It was nice and straight, a decent amateur's shot about 170 yards down the middle.

"Nice shot, Janet," Sofia said.

"Yes, a good start, I'd say," Enzo added.

Sofia stepped up next and set her tee and ball in the ground. Her shot rocketed about two hundred twenty yards down the middle. She stood for a moment, holding her finish, admiring it.

"Nice!" Enzo exclaimed. "I can imagine how good you were in high school."

Her attitude softened by her good tee shot, Sofia shrugged at him. "I don't get to play much anymore. I'm a little rusty. I used to drive a little farther."

"I'm sure you did. Boyfriend doesn't play?" Enzo asked as he set up for his turn.

"None of your business," Sofia answered, and stepped off the tee box to watch him swing.

Enzo focused down the fairway, apparently choosing his target and without a practice swing hit a perfect drive about 280 yards out into the middle.

Watching it, Sofia was embarrassed for herself. She knew golf better than he did?

"Wow," said Janet. Sofia jabbed her in the ribs.

"Let's go see if we can find those shots," Sofia said. "I think yours was slicing a little, Enzo." She climbed in their cart and looked at Janet with chagrin.

Three hours later, Sofia and Enzo walked side by side into the clubhouse chatting about their shots on the 18th. It had taken a few holes, but Enzo's skill and course etiquette had finally broken through her resistance. He was polite, complimented her and Janet on good shots, held the flag, helped rake bunkers, stood out of the way on the putting green, and was quiet during their shots. She'd seen much less admirable behavior from most men she'd played with since competing on the golf team in high school.

"Why didn't you tell me how good you were?" Sofia asked as they took stools at the tiny bar in the back of the golf shop.

"You didn't ask. And you didn't tell me how rusty you were."

Sofia slugged him in the arm. "That's not fair. I work 60 hours a week. And I live in a place where it rains 320 days a year. We don't tan in Seattle, we rust."

"Then while you're here, we should play a few more times," Enzo said, nodding to both women.

"I thought you were here to work, not golf," Janet said.

"Well, I didn't know I'd have such delightful golfing partners, or I'd have come here on vacation instead."

Sofia grimaced. He was trying too hard.

Enzo waved at the bartender who walked in from a back room, and continued. "I plan to work afternoons and evenings. The tasting rooms are open late. That's what I'm here to see."

The bartender approached, wiping his hands on a bar towel. "What'll it be, folks?"

"Pinot grigio," Janet ordered. "Local if possible."

"Do you carry any hard cider?" Sofia asked.

"No, sorry." The bartender shook his head. "Beer, wine and hard seltzer. Sodas, of course."

"I'll just take a local brew, then," Sofia said, a bit of a whine in her voice. "Whatever you recommend."

The bartender looked at Enzo. "And you?"

"I'll have a hard seltzer. Do you have grapefruit?"

Sofia shot him a look of disgust.

"What? What did I say?" Enzo sat back from her with a chuckle.

Sofia shook her head and looked away.

Enzo shrugged and turned to Janet. "And what do you do here?" he asked.

"I'm a banker. I make loans to wineries. You know, for equipment, marketing, working capital."

"Great, perhaps you can make some introductions for me."

Sofia listened as Enzo and Janet chatted happily for a while. Then she tuned them out and stared out the window and down the fairway. It looked like it stretched all the way to the horizon and the purple hills in the distance. It reminded her again how much she missed these wide, open spaces.

Six

THE HEAT OF THE DAY dissipated quickly up on the hill. Janet and Sofia had taken Rufus for a long walk through the vineyard earlier, and now he rested contentedly at their feet on the patio. He let out a big sigh, and Sofia mimicked him with one of her own.

"I forget sometimes how beautiful this is," she said, staring off across the tops of the vines. A light breeze fluttered the big grape leaves, shifting the kaleidoscope of light shining off of them from dozens of purples to dozens of greens in a silent dance. The air was warm but fresh, so dry it couldn't hold onto an odor. "Can you believe how lucky we were to grow up here?"

"Well," Janet replied. "You grew up here. I grew up down there." She pointed southeast toward town in the valley below.

"But you know what I mean," said Sofia. "It was fun playing golf with you again today."

"It's been too long. I think we were better in high school, though."

"You should come to Seattle sometime. We can go out to the peninsula and play. Lots of great courses out there," Sofia said, her gaze into the distance stuck as if she were in a trance.

"Yeah, maybe."

Sofia shook her head to release her stare and poured a little more wine into her glass. "What do you mean, 'maybe?'"

Janet paused a moment before answering. "Tell me about Thomas," she said. "Is there still a Thomas?"

Sofia sniffed. "Of course, there's still a Thomas. I told you, he had to go to Denver for a marketing meeting."

"It's been, what, three years since you met? Is anything really happening there?"

Sofia picked at the charcuterie plate, finally selecting a slice of sausage and bending down to hold it in front Rufus's nose. He gently picked it out of her fingers.

"We're busy with our careers," Sofia said. "But, yes, I think something's happening. We're learning about each other, figuring out what makes sense for us."

Janet laughed and flicked a dismissive wave with a hand. "What do you mean? 'What makes sense?' I want to hear about feelings, emotions, not 'what makes sense.'"

"Okay, let me be honest with you. But keep this to yourself." Sofia paused, parsing her next words. "I really don't know if he's committed to us anymore."

Janet nodded. "Well, how do you feel? Are you *in love* with him?"

"Yes, I love him."

"That's not what I asked. I asked if you are *in love* with him."

Sofia stuck a piece of cheese in her mouth, delaying her answer while she considered it. "I don't know. I guess I always thought that would come later, you know. As we got to know each other better."

She reached for the wine bottle and drizzled another ounce into her glass.

"You know being here reminds me of how I felt about Julio, as bad as that turned out. I've always wondered if that was just something you felt when you were too young to know better, or if that's something you could feel when you were grown up."

"You mean good old infatuation? Or lust? Which one drove the two of you out there on the golf course in the middle of the night?" Janet asked with a laugh.

Sofia looked stern. "You know nothing serious happened, right? I told you that."

"Sure, if you think running under the sprinklers naked is nothing." Janet giggled.

"You know what I mean. Nothing sexual happened. We were just playing."

"Honestly," Janet said. "I've never known if you're telling me everything."

"Like what? What else should I tell you?"

"I mean, did you want something else to happen? Did you like him that much?"

Sofia weighed that question too before answering. "I don't know. I don't think I knew then. I was only seventeen. Sex was just fantasy. But it didn't matter, since the groundskeeper caught us and then told the entire town, and Julio pretended that something more had happened. Like some sort of conquest. Boy, that was embarrassing."

Janet took a big gulp of wine and reached over for the bottle.

"Well then, Sofia," she said, "it's good that you and I are the only ones in town who remember anything about that."

"Geez, I hope you're right." Janet wrapped a piece of cheese in a sliver of prosciutto and popped it in her mouth.

"So, explain what it is you have against Enzo?" she asked. "He's damn good looking, obviously a great golfer, and seems to want to get along. Why are you being so difficult with him?"

"It doesn't really matter, Janet. I'm already in a committed relationship. I don't want Enzo to get any ideas. I mean we're stuck in this house together for my entire vacation."

"Maybe you're overestimating your irresistibility."

Sofia reached for a piece of cheese and threw it at Janet. It landed on the patio behind her, and Rufus got up to retrieve it. "I can't believe you said that. Whose friend are you anyway?"

"I know you better than anybody in the world," Janet answered. "I'd even argue that I know you better than Thomas does. And frankly, when I met him, I wondered how someone goes through life calling himself 'Thomas'—instead of 'Tom'—and not ironically."

Sofia chuckled and fed Rufus another piece of sausage.

A moment later, Enzo walked out of the house at the far end of the patio. Rufus stood up and waddled over to him. Enzo leaned down to scratch the dog's ear and then leaned against the railing, looking over the vineyard toward the west and the setting sun. He appeared to be oblivious to the women sitting on the other side.

"Hi! We're over here!" Janet called out to him, waving her arm in the air.

Sofia slapped her arm. "Shh. Damn you, Janet. I was enjoying our peace and quiet."

Enzo turned toward them and grinned. He followed Rufus back to their table.

"Oh, I'm sorry. I didn't know you were out here," he said. "I wasn't trying to ignore you."

"Come, sit down," Janet said. "We're just talking about your golf game. Tell me, how did you get so good?"

Sofia flashed her a dirty look, and if Enzo saw it, he

pretended he didn't. He nodded at Sofia, who faked a smile. He returned it with a sincere one.

"So good?" he answered Janet. "My game is half of what it used to be."

"I'd hate to imagine what it used to be," she said. "What do you mean?"

"I was on the circuit, the professional tour in Argentina. A while ago. But I finally realized I'd never make the PGA in the U.S. I just wasn't good enough, and I decided I needed to make a living. Gave up the game."

Sofia tried to hide her interest in their conversation, but she couldn't resist turning her head to look at him. He sat down between them and waved an arm at the vineyard stretching out below them.

"This reminds me so much of Mendoza. I could feel at home here."

"Did you grow up in the vineyards there?" Janet asked.

"Yes, my father tended the vines for one of the large growers. I spent my entire childhood running down the rows, throwing sticks for my dogs. When the owner died, he deeded the property to my dad. I guess he attributed all of his success to my father's excellent care. Dad started making his own wine about ten years ago. When I returned home from the golf tour, I went right to work for him, a chance to learn viticulture from the best in Argentina."

Janet kept up her end of the conversation, while Sofia sulked. "And you know Sofia's brother?"

"Yes, we play golf together," Enzo said. He turned to Sofia. "He's very good, you know."

"Oh, of course I know," she said. "He'd never let me forget it."

She returned Enzo's look and lost her resolve to stay cool. His dark eyes smiled at her, and he looked sincere. She grinned in spite of herself.

"Well, he's been a great friend to me. Not that I've always deserved it. He helped me convince my dad that I should quit pruning vines and ratchet up our marketing."

"What's wrong with pruning vines? It takes skill and precision. Yields, sugar content, well, everything depends on it," Sofia said. She watched his expression turn serious.

"Ah, yes. But if I'm going to take over the business someday, I had to get out of the vineyard and into the office. I think my father would prefer to believe he'll live forever, and I won't have to learn what he does in there."

Sofia's cellphone buzzed, vibrating the table and startling all of them. Enzo pointed to it, and Sofia looked at the screen.

"Oh," she said. "Sorry, I have to get this. Janet, could you get our guest a glass? Perhaps we should introduce him to some quality Walla Walla wine."

Sofia picked up the phone and walked off the edge of the patio into the garden that separated it from the vineyard below.

"Hello!"

"Hello, Sofia? What took you so long to answer?" Thomas sounded impatient.

"I'm sitting out on the patio with Janet. What took you so long to call? It's been three days. Where are you? It sounds quiet there."

"I'm on my hotel room balcony, looking out at the mountains. It's very peaceful."

"I never thought of Denver as peaceful," she said. "How is it going? The meetings?"

"Oh, busy, you know. Marketing meetings. You know how they are. Boring and contentious at the same time."

"But it's going okay?"

"Oh, fine. fine. How are things there? Getting any relaxation or are you taking work calls?"

Sofia walked to the edge of the garden and turned to

watch Janet and Enzo on the patio. They were getting along very well.

"Thomas, you know it's always you who interrupts our vacation with business calls. No, I actually played a round of golf today."

"Great. How was your game? ... Uh, hold on a minute, someone just came in ... ."

Sofia could hear a woman's voice, her words muffled.

"What's going on there?" Sofia asked.

"Oh, nothing," Thomas answered. "Look, I have to go. I hope you're having a great time. I'll try to call tomorrow."

Before she could answer, the call disconnected. Sofia pulled the phone from her ear and stared at the screen. What was that all about? If he was on the balcony of his room, why was a woman talking in the background? Sofia tucked the phone in her back pocket and walked back up to the patio with Enzo and Janet watching her.

"I suppose that was Thomas," Janet said flatly.

"Good guess," Sofia answered, plopping back down in her chair.

"Thomas?" Enzo asked. "Is that your boyfriend?"

Janet answered for her. "Ostensibly. I'm not that sure, though. Sofia, what did he have to say?"

"Not much. But it sounded like things are going well. I'm glad he went. It's for our future, you know. He's up for a big promotion. This might help move things along."

Janet snorted. "Oh, I'm sure it will." She turned to Enzo. "This Thomas ... He's been dating Sofia for three years now, and, well, just let me say—"

Sofia cut her off. "Enough Janet. That's enough." She faced Enzo. "My friend has never cared for Thomas. I'd chock it up to jealousy, but ..." She reached over and lifted Janet's arm to show Enzo the big diamond ring on Janet's left hand.

"Right." Janet laughed. "What have I got to be jealous

of? I'm happily married, happy in my work, love my hometown." She paused and put a hand on Enzo's arm. "Look, all I have to say is if you were to meet Thomas, well, I think you'd wonder too." She theatrically lifted her eyebrows and her wine glass.

"Janet, I said that's enough." Sofia's voice was testy.

"So, this man is okay with you running off to Walla Walla without him?" Enzo asked Sofia. "Doesn't he worry about what handsome men you might run into?"

Sofia feigned disdain. "I don't suppose you're referring to yourself? No, he's not worried. And he doesn't know you're here."

"Oh, that's interesting. You didn't tell him?"

Sofia ignored the question. "We're very happy together. Committed."

"Engaged?" he asked. "When's the wedding?"

Sofia lowered her voice. "We haven't gotten that far."

Enzo turned to Janet. "How long did you say it has been?"

Sofia answered. "Only three years."

Enzo laughed. "Only? I have known vineyards to take that long to establish, but not love."

It was Sofia's turn to laugh. "Well, you're Latin. I guess things happen faster for you. Your hot blood and all. Perhaps it's my mother's cold Scandinavian blood that's my problem."

Enzo tilted his head down and peered at her under his eyebrows. "Perhaps he's not the right one."

Sofia blushed at his intense look. "I certainly don't think you're in a position to judge that."

Enzo sat back and smiled apologetically. "No, of course not. I apologize." He reached over and briefly laid his hand on Sofia's forearm. He sat back again. "Let's start over."

He waved his arm out at the darkening vineyard and looked up at the stars that were starting to peep out in the sky. "It is certainly a lovely evening, isn't it, ladies?"

Seven

Most of the nearly forty wine tasting rooms in down-town Walla Walla didn't open before 11 a.m., but Francois met Sofia at the door of his at 10.

"Sofia!" he exclaimed, his arms wide open. She stepped into his bear hug and fought back tears.

"Oh, Frenchie, I have missed you," she mumbled into his soft, round shoulder. She sniffed and stood back to look at him. "And you don't look a day older."

"A few pounds heavier," he said, laughing and patting his protruding tummy.

"It wouldn't be you without this," she said, adding a pat of her own.

"I'm so glad you called," he said. "Are you back in town? Looking for a job? I could use a good server."

"I don't think you could afford me. I've gotten used to the big city salary, I'm afraid."

"Sit here and tell me all about it." Francois pulled a

stool away from his serving counter, and Sofia hopped into it. "And you have to try my new mourvèdre."

He slipped behind the counter and pulled a corked bottle out from a low cabinet. Sofia watched her old friend inspect a wine glass in the light of the bar and pour her a couple of ounces. Francois had purchased grapes from her parents from as far back as she remembered, right up to when they sold the vineyard. He'd always been like an uncle to her, attending her birthday parties and graduation ceremonies, and letting her help with the crush, even when she was too young to contribute much but big enough to be in the way. At sixty, he still moved with the weightlessness of a much younger man, although his thinning hair had turned silver. Sofia wondered if his famously prodigious wine consumption had anything to do with his rigor. As soon as she was old enough to understand, he had preached that wine was an age-defying potion more potent than the fountain of youth.

"I didn't know you were doing mourvèdre," she said, tipping the glass up to breathe in a big lungful of its nose. "Where are you getting the grapes?"

"Why don't you taste it and see if you can tell me," he said, leaning forward with his hands on the bar, waiting for her verdict.

"Gosh, Frenchie, I think I've been gone too long. No palate left." She tipped the glass again for a taste and swirled the tiny bit of liquid in her mouth before swallowing it.

"But what do you think?"

"Wonderful," she said. "What's the alcohol content? 13?"

"Good guess. It's 13.2," he said. "You haven't lost it entirely. Now tell me what you're up to in that big city you've grown so fond of."

Carefully choosing her words, Sofia fashioned a description of her job and her life in Seattle that sounded as upbeat as possible without bending the truth too much. No one wanted to hear her complain, not even an old family friend like Frenchie. As she struggled to put her job and her relationship into the best light possible, her mind took off on another track. If making her life sound good was so hard to do, why didn't she do something about it?

"A fiancé?" Francois lifted his bushy eyebrows. "I don't think your father told me anything about that."

"I don't think he's too crazy about Thomas."

"Thomas, huh. But you're in love, right, honey?"

Sofia opened her fingers and waggled her hand. "More or less. I'm not sure I'm any more excited about it than my parents are," she said. "Not since he cancelled his plans to come with me again. For the third time in a row."

Francois slapped the counter with his palm, making Sofia jump. "That won't do! Hey, I know just the thing for you. We're about to harvest, and I'd love to have you come and help with crush. There's a whole bunch of wineries that'll be crushing at the same time. You can look around. See if anyone catches your fancy." He wiggled his eyebrows.

"Frenchie. I know every man in this town. I grew up here, remember."

"Oh, but there are so many more wineries now, and so many new vintners. You don't know half of them."

"Well, it does sound a lot more fun than selling cider," she said, holding out her glass for another sample.

Francois reached for the mourvèdre and held it up, questioning if she wanted more of the same. Sofia nodded and he poured again.

"I know you're trying to make it sound like you're happy over there in Seattle," he said. "But I wonder if that's true. Don't you like what you're doing?"

Sofia sipped some wine and considered how to answer. "I do," she said. "As much as anyone does, I guess."

"I'm not sure about that. I love what I do. I've never wanted to do anything else."

Sofia watched as he turned away, picked up a rag, and started to shine the glass doors on the cabinets behind the bar. He looked happy.

"Well, I'll admit," she said. "I miss working with wine."

"What about it do you miss?"

"The romance of it. The subtleties of every vintage. The heritage."

She leaned forward with her elbow on the counter and her chin resting on her hand.

"And being outside," she continued. "Even in the winter. I'd rather be back here working in the vineyard, but when Dad decided to sell, I didn't have much choice. And I guess I think people still remember what happened with Julio that summer."

Francois faced her and frowned.

"Julio? Who is Julio?"

Sofia laughed. "He was our Argentinian exchange student. The fact that you don't remember him makes me very relieved. I thought … ." She waved her hand to dismiss the subject. Apparently, she could finally let it go. "Oh, never mind."

"Speaking of Argentina," Francois said, offering her more wine, which she declined, "you have a guest at the house, I hear. A man your brother knows from Mendoza?"

"Yes, trust me. It was not my idea. I was coming for a little R&R and to see Rufus, not to host some Latin would-be Romeo."

"Well, this guest of yours is coming by this morning to talk about our tasting room business." Francois glanced at his watch. "I guess he's trying to learn marketing for his family's winery."

"Oh, Jeez. Everywhere I go—" Sofia started to complain, but Francois interrupted, pointing at the front door.

"I'm guessing this is him now."

Sofia turned to see Enzo walk in. He grinned brightly.

"I didn't know you'd be here," he said. "What a surprise!"

Francois slid around the end of the counter to shake Enzo's hand. "You must be Enzo. *Bienvenido*! I guess you know Sofia here."

"Indeed, I do. We had a lovely evening under the stars on the patio last night." Enzo faced Sofia and bowed slightly. "I'm enjoying her hospitality very much."

"That's kind of you to say," Sofia said, hopping off her bar stool and reaching for her purse. "I'll leave you two to discuss business. I've got some errands I need to run for Dad."

Enzo stepped forward to kiss Sofia's cheek. She blushed and turned to catch Francois winking at Enzo.

"You don't have to leave, Sofia," Francois said. "I'm sure there are no state secrets about to be divulged."

Sofia shook her head. "Thanks for the tasting, Francois. I guess I'll see you at the house later, Enzo."

"I am looking forward to it. I am making dinner tonight, by the way. Is *coq au vin* suitable? And is Janet coming again?"

Sofia was surprised. *Coq au vin*? Would he really go to that trouble?

"Yes, uh … uh, *coq au vin* will be … uh, great," she stammered. She recovered her poise. "But, no, Janet headed to the Tri-Cities with her husband today. She won't be back in time."

Enzo's grin widened even more, and she avoided his eyes. He was getting more attractive every time she saw him. It wasn't fair.

"So, it will be just you and me," he said happily.

"And Rufus," Sofia added, walking as far around Enzo as she could without looking rude.

"Of course. I'd never forget Rufus."

Sofia fled for the door, feeling Enzo's and Francois's

eyes on her back. Just as she slipped out, she heard Francois's harsh whisper to Enzo: "You could do worse."

"Don't I know it," she heard him respond.

Eight

THE CAST-IRON SCONCES ON TWO sides of the patio provided a soft light, barely illuminating the walls that surrounded the dining table on two sides. The pink rays of the sunset reflected off the bottom of low clouds in the west, remnants of an afternoon thunderstorm, and painted the vineyard below in a rosy glow.

When Sofia walked out onto the patio for dinner, Enzo was lighting two tall candles on the table, which he had set with cloth napkins, crystal wine glasses, and a little bowl of flowers. Two flutes of champagne awaited them along with a decanter that aired the evening's pinot noir.

Enzo looked up as Sofia stood, amazed at the elegance he and the evening sky had conjured on the rustic patio. He smiled, and she knew immediately that he appreciated the effort she had put into dressing for dinner.

She wore the red knit dress that showed off her slim figure and her simple diamond pendant, and her hair was swept back into a soft, slightly messy French braid.

Enzo put down the lighter, as if afraid he would set something on fire accidentally while he stared at her. "Wow. You look beautiful. This is for me?"

Sofia nodded. "I thought if you were going to the trouble of *coq au vin*, the least I could do is dress for dinner."

Enzo exhaled. "Well, thank you." He pulled out a chair for her.

"Sit. Please. I'll get the soup."

"This is incredible," she said, accepting the seat. "You managed all of this and you've only been in the house for a couple of days?"

"Well, Rufus helped," Enzo said. "Turns out he knows where everything is. He even helped me pick out the wine."

He disappeared back into the kitchen with Rufus trotting after him. For a moment, Sofia considered the possibility that he had charmed Rufus as much as he was charming her, and had, indeed, gotten the dog to help make dinner.

The meal was exquisitely French, which surprised Sofia. Yes, she knew the entré would be *coq au vin,* but Enzo had stuck to a traditional Gallic presentation of soup first, followed by his entré, then a palate-cleansing salad, a small plate of cheeses, and finally, a dessert of *pot au crème* topped with a few raspberries. Each course was presented in just the right proportion to be satisfying, but not over-whelming.

"I don't know when I've ever had such a fine meal," Sofia said, spooning out the last of the *crème* from her dish. "I think if I die now, I'll know I've not been deprived of the very best in French cuisine."

Enzo smiled his thanks and offered his wine glass for a toast. "And here's to serendipity. I had no idea my visit to Estados Unidos would be so full of pleasurable moments."

"You are too kind," Sofia said. "I was such a bitch—"

"No more of that," Enzo gently cut her off. "It was perfectly understandable. I was early. I was not invited by you. And I probably come on a little too strong with most introductions. It's my country habits. Mendoza may be a famous wine region, but we're still mostly farmers."

He stood up to remove their plates, but Sofia reached out and put her hand on his forearm.

"No," she said. "I insist on cleaning up. You made an incredible meal and I will do the dishes. Put those down."

Enzo did as he was told. He laid the dishes on the cabinet by the door and returned to the table. He picked up the bottle of wine and poured a little more in Sofia's glass before sitting down.

"It is so fortunate your parents kept the house when they sold the vineyards," he said, sighing a bit as he sat. "It's so beautiful here."

"Yes. I hope I can come back here someday. It's my favorite place in the whole world."

They sat in silence for a few minutes. Sofia felt oddly comfortable next to this man whom she was so determined to avoid. He seemed to appreciate the quiet countryside and the vineyard view as much as she did. They watched the sunset colors fade on the horizon.

"Is it possible we could play some golf tomorrow morning? I think I could give you a tip or two to help your game," Enzo finally spoke up as dusk hit the patio.

Sofia laughed. "So, you think my game needs help?"

"Everyone's game needs help. Tiger Woods had a coach. But I had fun out there with you the other day. And you have a lovely swing."

"That's very flattering. But don't you have to work?"

"My next appointment with a vintner isn't until tomorrow evening."

"Okay, then. I'd love to play."

"Great. I already made a tee time. We'll be the first on the course."

Enzo paused, and he looked away, as if he had suddenly been hit by a bout of melancholy. He stared at the wine in his glass.

"What is it?" Sofia asked.

"I need to apologize for springing this visit on you. I understand you didn't plan on coming here and spending your vacation with a complete stranger. But thanks for sharing your home with me. You are a beautiful hostess, and I'm so grateful to your brother for this chance to meet you."

"Ha! I'm the one who should apologize. It was a such a surprise when Thomas told me he wasn't coming with me, and then my mother told me you were coming. You see, I have a bit of a troubled history with male house guests here, and I had flashbacks like I was going through that again."

Enzo peered at her in the waning light. "Want to give me a clue? What happened?"

Sofia thought about not answering, but the intimacy of the setting seemed to beg for a confessional.

"It was long ago. I was still in high school," she explained. "My father's friend in Argentina—the guy who helped Michael get started there—sent his son my age to stay with us one summer to learn a little about American viticulture from my dad."

Enzo guessed: "And you didn't get along."

Sofia shook her head. "No, actually, we got along a little too well. It all ended with a nighttime episode on the golf course, the police were called, and this being a small town, well … "

"… and pretty soon everyone knew," Enzo finished for her.

Sofia nodded, a sardonic smile forming. In the retelling this many years later, it seemed a lot less scandalous than it had before.

"You don't have to say any more," Enzo said.

But Sofia continued anyway. "It was really so innocent, but Julio didn't want anyone to think it was. He built it up, embellishing with lies … you can imagine what lies … and I could see people looking at my belly for the next six months. I couldn't wait to get out of here and go to Seattle for college. I even graduated from high school a semester early, just so I could leave."

"I'm sure no one else remembers it though."

Sofia looked at him appreciatively. "Turns out you're right. I guess when you're seventeen, you're sure you're invisible until suddenly, everyone's staring at you and you want to hide."

"I feel the need to apologize for my countryman. Obviously, I don't know this Julio, but—"

Sofia stopped him. "No, no. This has nothing to do with you. It was silly for me to connect the two of you. This is something I should have gotten over a long time ago."

Enzo stood up and reached out for her hand. "Have you ever walked through a vineyard at night? It's the most incredible place in the world under the stars."

Sofia smiled and rose, letting him hold her hand. "Yes, I have. And I agree."

They stepped into the garden and passed through to the vineyard, and Rufus followed them. As they walked down between the vines, Sofia looked up at Enzo's face. It was hard to see his expression in the waning light, but she sensed he was at peace. Rufus ran ahead, chasing some kind of rodent, and then came bounding back to them and nudged Sofia's hand.

She looked down at him. "You didn't really want to catch that critter, did you?" she said, patting the top of his head. She looked up at the stars as they turned to walk back toward the patio.

"This is what I miss," she said quietly. "You never see stars like this in Seattle. Maybe Venus, sometimes the Big

Dipper. But there are too many lights to see anything else."

"I wish I could show you the stars in the Southern Hemisphere." Enzo nearly whispered too, and Sofia realized they were still holding hands. It had happened so naturally, and now she decided not to resist it. "You have your Big Dipper and North Star. We have the Southern Cross. The air in Mendoza is so clear that the Milky Way sparkles like a belt of shining jewels."

Sofia sighed. "Maybe I'll come down to visit Michael sometime."

Enzo stopped and Sofia stopped with him. "And me?" he said, circling to face her and look into her eyes.

"Yes," she whispered. "And you."

"I will wish upon a star for that to happen, Sofia."

He bent his head down and Sofia closed her eyes and lifted hers, anticipating the soft touch of his lips. Just as their lips met, a raspy jingle rang out from the patio. Startled by the sound, they stepped apart.

"It's my phone," Sofia said. "That's probably Thomas." She dropped Enzo's hand and stepped back toward the patio. "I'm sorry. I have to get that. He's been so hard to get ahold of."

She could barely see his face, but Enzo's voice rang with disappointment. "Of course," he said. "Thomas. I forgot."

Sofia ran up the hill with Rufus trotting ahead of her. She picked up the phone and went inside without turning look back at Enzo. She knew that if she did, the hitch in her voice would betray her.

Nine

THEY MET A LITTLE AFTER sunrise the next morning at Wine Valley Country Club, and Sofia was glad Enzo didn't ask about the call from Thomas. She would have had to lie and tell him that it was fine. Good, even. Maybe great.

It hadn't been. Once again, Thomas had been in a hurry, and when she asked what was keeping him so busy well into the evening—it was nearly nine o'clock, after all—he scolded her for being suspicious.

"I'm not suspicious," she replied. And truth was, she hadn't been until he suggested it. Then she worried. Was there someone in Denver on the new marketing team that had caught his eye? She couldn't imagine that. He hardly seemed to have time for her, let alone another woman right then.

The call had ended unhappily, with Sofia feeling guilty about what had just about happened in the vineyard with Enzo and with Thomas angry.

She didn't want to share that with Enzo, especially since he had to know she was as attracted to him as he seemed to her. Instead, Enzo acted as if he had forgotten the walk through the vines. Perhaps she would get over this silly infatuation if he quit encouraging it. She could hope.

The morning was perfect for golf. The air was still. They teed off on the first hole as the first rays of sunlight burst over the low hills behind them. The tall, golden grass that covered the ridge to the left sparkled with morning dew. Sofia spied a coyote running at the edge of the fairway and pointed. Enzo saw it just before it disappeared into the deep thatch.

Being more familiar with the course, Sofia drove the golf cart, and Enzo didn't seem to mind. Thomas, Sofia reflected to herself, had a fit if she suggested she drive. It was as if he thought it threatened his masculinity or, at least, his masculine reputation.

The damp greens held their approach shots nicely, and they had the course nearly to themselves. With their long drives and a few good putts, they put the first nine holes behind them in little more than ninety minutes, and as they made the turn to the second nine, Sofia worried that the lovely morning was passing too quickly. Just as the thought occurred to her, Enzo echoed it.

"Let's slow down," he said. "I don't have anywhere I have to be until later today. Why don't we ditch the cart and walk the back nine?"

"My thought exactly!" she said.

She pulled the electric cart up to the cart barn, and they walked away a few minutes later with pull-carts.

"This is so much more like it!" Enzo said. "You know, we walk more in Argentina. Not many courses even have golf carts."

"So that's why you're in such good shape," Sofia said. "I hope I can walk this far. I don't think I've walked nine holes in more than five years. Since I was in college."

"We don't have to rush. There isn't anyone behind us for a few holes."

Sofia had honors on the tenth tee, having beat Enzo on the ninth hole. She swung easily off the tee and stepped aside for Enzo's turn. His tee shot was a few yards longer, but her second shot hit the green while his skidded off to the right across the cart path into a patch of scrubby ground covering. She putted in for a birdie while he looked for his ball, and then she walked over to help him search. She found it nearly buried under the foliage and laughed.

"Oh, I don't envy you," she said.

Enzo walked to the ball and shrugged. "I've seen worse."

He pulled out an iron, and without hesitating a moment, hit the ball out of the scrub in a high arc that landed on the green and rolled into the hole.

"I can't believe that!" Sofia cried. She reached over and raised her arm for a high-five. Enzo slapped her hand and walked on the green to retrieve his ball.

"I said I'd seen worse," he said, walking back to their pull carts and trying to hide his grin.

"You're a big show-off!" Sofia grabbed the handle of her pull-cart and led the way to the next tee box.

"Actually," he said, following close, "that was luck. I had no idea what I was doing."

As the morning stretched on, their progress slower now that they were walking, they laughed and talked, taking their time to line up long, winding putts and congratulating each other on good shots. Sofia tried to remember the last time she had enjoyed a round so much, and decided it probably was back when she played with Julio that summer, before he betrayed her and was sent home in infamy. Playing with Thomas was certainly no joy.

Sofia noticed that Enzo was keeping his distance, approaching her only for high-fives and a quick, platonic hug on the eighteenth green. A few times, she caught him watching her intently, but he looked away quickly, as if he knew she had noticed. It seemed that he was working hard to accept his limited place in her life.

Leaving the eighteenth hole, they walked with their carts toward their cars in the lot, reaching Enzo's rental first. Sofia waited while he loaded his clubs in the trunk.

"I'll take your cart back," she said. "I know you need to clean up for your afternoon meetings."

"Thanks," he said, accepting the favor. "I had a great time out there, Sofia. Your game isn't far off. You just need to play more."

"Don't I know it. But, yes, it was fun. Thanks."

She started to walk away, but he called out after her. "About last night …"

She turned to face him.

"I'm sorry, I should have said this earlier. I forgot about Thomas. Maybe it was the stars, maybe your dress, maybe the wine. I don't know, but I apologize. I don't want you to think I'm another Julio."

Sofia smiled at the irony. She was just thinking that in some wonderful ways, he was another Julio. But this time, she would be careful not to let those things seduce her. Perhaps if she kept thoughts of Thomas on the top of her mind, she could maintain a safe distance between them.

"No, I'm sorry," she answered. "I got carried away. There's something about a vineyard at dusk that makes me forget my real life. It was my fault."

Enzo took a step toward her. "So, Thomas was okay? Everything going well for him?"

"Yes. It was a short call. He seems really busy. We'll talk again tonight."

"Good. I'll be back late. Don't wait up."

Sofia laughed. "I wasn't going to."

She walked toward her car to load her clubs and looked

back to watch him wave and drive away.

"Oh, golf gods," she whispered, looking up into the cloudless sky. "Give me strength to resist this. Get me back to Seattle before it's too late."

She pulled out her cell phone and texted Thomas:

Thinking about you … will call tonight … hope all is going well. XO

Ten

Sofia waited for Janet at a table in one of the downtown coffee shops close to her friend's bank and considered filling the time with a quick call to Thomas. It would be good to hear his voice. It would bring her back to earth after the high-flying emotions of the past twenty-four hours.

"Let's see." She thought out loud. "Denver is only an hour ahead of us. So, it's only three o'clock there." She decided it would be better to wait until the end of the workday. He barely had time to talk to her in the evenings. He certainly wouldn't stop work to chat in the middle of the afternoon.

She put the phone down just as Janet walked in.

"Whatcha drinking?" Janet asked, setting her purse down on the chair next to Sofia.

"Iced coffee."

"I guess I'll do the same." Janet walked up to the counter, and Sofia studied her from behind. Her friend had put on a few pounds since their high-school golf team days, but she was still trim and fit. The modest business suit she wore with low, classic pumps fit perfectly, and her messy strawberry blond braid bespoke businesswoman too busy to be fussy.

"I'm glad you called," Sofia said when Janet returned. "I was trying to figure out what to do this afternoon."

Janet sat down and pulled the paper covering off the straw with her teeth. "Well, I don't have a lot of time, but I want to see you as much as I can before you leave. Usually I don't take coffee breaks in the afternoon, but we're not that busy right now."

"How was the trip to the Tri-Cities?"

"Fine. About as exciting as you'd expect. I met with some winery owners and Jason looked at a new combine."

They lived in town, now, but Janet's husband was a wheat farmer who had grown up in the business on his family's farm. He was accustomed to spending a half-million dollars or more at a time on a piece of machinery, a concept that had once blown Janet's mind. "That is until I saw what wineries spend on fermentation tanks, distillers, and bottlers," she told Sofia. "Now those numbers don't wow me anymore."

Janet glanced at the door, and Sofia turned to see what she was looking at. "Are you expecting someone?"

"Yes." Janet looked sheepish. "I'll be honest. I talked with one of my vintners the other day, and he said they're looking for a new marketing person for the wine region. I told him about you." She glanced at the door again and grinned. "Oh, here he is now."

"Hi, Will!" Janet waved and Sofia turned to see a middle-aged man dressed in winemaker's attire—jeans, khaki shirt, and sturdy boots. All he was missing was an apron.

Sofia whispered to Janet. "I'm not dressed for this. You should have asked."

Ignoring her, Janet stood to give Will a hug and introduce him to Sofia.

"I know your father well," Will said, shaking Sofia's hand. "Great man, great viticulturalist."

"Thanks. I'll give him your regards when he's back from their trip."

Janet motioned for Will to sit with them. "Can I get you a coffee?"

Will shook his head. "No, no. I've just got a couple of minutes." He turned to Sofia. "Janet tells me you may be looking for a way back into the wine business."

Sofia laughed. "Uh, this is the first I've heard of it."

Janet shook her head. "You said the other day that you miss wine—"

Will cut her off with a dismissive wave. "Tell me what you're doing now, Sofia."

"I'm working at a brewery in Seattle. We recently brought out a new hard cider, and I've been trying to build our market presence."

"And how's that going?"

Sofia frowned. "Not especially well. I think the timing was bad. Just when we thought there was room for another cider brand, consumers decided to switch to hard seltzers."

Will looked surprised. "No market research?"

"Oh, no. Plenty," Sofia said. "But between the time we got the data and got the product ready for the market, things changed."

Will nodded. Sofia imagined he understood how quickly beverage tastes and trends could change, especially for products marketed to millennials. She could have faulted the market research firm for failing to see the turn to seltzers, but blaming others for your failures was no way to impress.

"Are you interested in returning to the wine country?" he asked. "I sense some ambivalence." He glanced at Janet.

"I guess it is something I think about. But, I haven't—"

Will interrupted again. It appeared he was in a hurry, just as he said. "What appeals to you about wine?"

Sofia thought for a moment, but Will's impatient expression pushed her to answer quickly. "It's more steeped in heritage and tradition. The thing about the beer business is it's so trendy. One day it's all about ales and craft brews, then it's cider, and now, like I say, the beer drinking public is turning to seltzers. Fewer calories, I guess."

"Doesn't the wine business seem staid in comparison? Old school?"

"I don't think of viticulture or winemaking as staid. There's plenty of experimentation with technologies and new blends. It's just that it doesn't seem that it's so obsessed with changing fads."

"I agree with you totally," Will said. He placed both palms flat on the table, as if to lift himself from his chair. "I'm glad that Janet got us together. But I think we're looking for someone with a few more connections in the area—more recent ones, that is. I'd suggest you come back here, spend some time in marketing for one of our bigger producers, and in a couple of years, let's talk again. I'm sure Janet has her ear to the ground and can let you know when something's open."

Will stood. "I've got to run. I'll see you around, Janet. Good luck, Sofia."

He held out his hand to her. She stood up and took it. The shake was anything but warm, and moments later, Will was gone.

Sofia sat back down hard enough that she stung her tailbone. "Well, that was embarrassing," she said, frowning at her friend.

"What do you mean? You did great."

"I wasn't looking for an interview. Come on, Janet, let me run my own life."

"I'm not trying to run your life. I just want you to come back here." Janet glanced at her watch. "Oh, I've only got a minute."

"Janet," Sofia's voice was argumentative. "There's a big world out there. Walla Walla isn't the only great place with vineyards and wineries. I love coming home and seeing you. But even if I leave the brewery, I'm getting married. Thomas will never agree to move to Walla Walla."

"Would you move if it weren't for him?"

"That won't happen."

"How about Argentina?"

Sofia laughed. "Don't be silly."

Janet stood up and pulled her purse onto her shoulder.

"So, I'll see you tonight, right? A little wine tasting for old times' sake?"

Janet nodded and smiled. "I can't wait!"

Eleven

THE SIDEWALKS WERE CROWDED, EVEN on a weekday evening, but then, it was summer, and the tourist season was peaking. Strolling arm-in-arm with Janet, weaving among the milling oenophiles, Sofia could see that Janet's boast about the town booming was no exaggeration.

"This is the new place I wanted you to try." Janet steered Sofia around a family that nearly blocked the entrance as they argued about what tasting room to try next.

"These guys have been producing for only about five years, but they're doing some really fine Rhone blends," Janet said, introducing her new favorite winery. She made a beeline for a couple of empty stools at the tasting bar.

"And besides, they have stools up at the tasting counter. I appreciate that after a long day at work."

Sofia hoisted herself up onto the stool and watched the server behind the bar lean over and kiss Janet on both cheeks. Was cheek-kissing replacing handshakes out here in Eastern Washington the same way wine had replaced beer over the past couple of decades?

"Nice to see you, Janet," the server said. "You haven't been out much this summer, have you?"

Janet shook her head, despondently. "Too much work, Tim. But it's slowing down now." She pointed at Sofia. "This is my best friend from high school, Sofia. She lives in Seattle now."

The server reached out a hand to Sofia. Apparently only some people warranted the cheek kiss.

"You thinking of moving back?" he asked.

"Someday, maybe," Sofia said. She wondered how many more times she'd answer that question before she left. "But I've got a job and a fiancé in Seattle."

"Plenty of jobs here, Sofia." The server winked at her. "Plenty of alternative fiancés, too."

Sofia laughed. "I'm sure you're right. What are we tasting tonight?"

"Let me choose a couple for you. I already know just what Janet likes." The server walked away, and Sofia regarded his trim frame as he pulled a half-dozen glasses and started pouring tastes from different bottles.

"So, everyone knows you in this business now?" Sofia asked, still staring at the server, mesmerized by his graceful motion.

"Not everyone," Janet said. "Some of the big wineries have relationships with banks in Seattle and Denver. But most of the little guys come to us. I'm guessing we won't be paying for any tastings tonight."

"Great perk!" Sofia said, finally pulling her eyes away from the young man's frame. "I am really jealous. It seems like you've really figured things out. I didn't think any of us would end up back here when we left for college."

Janet smiled past her as the server returned with a tray of tastings.

"Here are three of our blends," he said, placing three glasses in front of Sofia. "Janet is familiar with them, but perhaps you want to test your palate and tell us what you think the varietals are?"

"I appreciate the challenge, Tim, but I'm afraid my palate is a little rusty," she said.

"Well, give these a try and wave me down when you're ready for a full glass."

Sofia handed him a credit card, but he put up his hand to refuse it. "We don't charge our friends here, Sofia. Enjoy. I'll be back to check on you."

"I guess you were right." Sofia held up the first glass to Janet for a toast. "Cheers! I'm in the mood for some great free wine."

Sofia took a sip. The dark red liquid surprised her. It was full-bodied, but it stung her tongue just a bit, as if it was peppered. "Mmmmm," she said, contended. "I'm not even going to try to guess what's in here. I'm just going to drink it!"

Settling in, Sofia pulled out her cellphone again and texted Thomas. She didn't want him to call while they were out. He'd scold her for being out late or slurring her words.

Can't call tonight. Out with Janet. I'll talk to you tomorrow.

Sofia put her phone away and looked around at the other patrons in the tasting room. As her eyes surveyed the scene near the front window, Janet elbowed her and pointed to the back of the room. "Well, look who's here!" she said. "Your nemesis."

Sofia followed Janet's eyes to where Enzo sat with an older man at a table in the back, facing her. He met her eyes and waved, but he returned immediately to his conversation. Sofia felt Janet watching her.

"Wait a minute, sister," Janet said. "I just saw that look you gave each other. What is happening here?"

Sofia feigned ignorance. "What are you talking about? What look?"

"Don't try to fool me. I know you too well. You've changed your mind about our new Argentinian friend?"

Sofia's crooked smile spread as a blush covered her cheeks. "He's definitely growing on me. We get along."

Janet leaned forward to try to catch her eye. "And?"

"And nothing." Sofia tried to relax the smile off her face. "Except we almost kissed the other night."

"I knew it! I'm not easily fooled, Sofia. So, what now?"

"Nothing, Janet. I'm engaged. I said we *almost* kissed. But I pulled myself together and took Thomas's phone call instead."

Janet laughed. "You mean a phone call interrupted you? What would have happened if Thomas hadn't called right then?"

Sofia took another sip and felt her body relaxing. She leaned forward with her elbows on the bar and rested her forehead on her free hand. "I don't know. I really don't know," she said.

Janet waited for her to continue.

"But don't read too much into it," Sofia said. "It was the wine, the sunset, the accent, you know. The romance of it all. I know what was happening, and it wasn't real."

"But—"

"No buts, Janet." Sofia dropped her hand and turned to her friend. "I want to change the subject. Really. I'm marrying Thomas. I'm going back to Seattle, going back to my job, and getting married. So, let's drop it, okay?"

"Okay!" Janet was grinning. "I'll drop it. But I can't really think of anything better to talk about."

Sofia laughed with her, and they simultaneously drained their glasses and reached for their next one.

Twelve

THE LATE AFTERNOON SUN THREW a thin ray of bright light across the kitchen floor through the north-facing window. If it hadn't, Sofia wouldn't have walked over to pull the blinds closed, and she wouldn't have noticed Enzo standing in the doorway to the dining room, his arms crossed, leaning against the jamb. She realized he must have seen her minutes before, as she was dancing, apron on and chef's knife in hand, to the ancient tunes of Abba. The music blared from the cheap boom-box her mother kept in the kitchen, convinced that no one needed high-quality sound if all they were going to listen to was sixties and seventies pop music.

"What are you doing?" Sofia stopped, still holding the big knife as if it would shield her from embarrassment.

"Watching you dance. You look so happy." He grinned, but he didn't budge from the door frame.

"Well, I had a great day today. Saw some old friends.

Went to the driving range to work on my game a little." Sofia wondered why she was delivering this stream of excuses for being content. "Thanks for your tips yesterday. I think it helped."

"Very welcome," Enzo said, still leaning and grinning.

Sofia started to blush. She moved around the kitchen island and resumed her work. She tipped up a freshly husked corn cob on end and sliced down, cutting the kernels off in perfectly matched blocks of three rows at a time.

"And I love to cook." She blabbed on. "I'm cooking you some realio, trulio American food. A Cajun vegetable dish. Lots of butter. I hope that's okay. And we're having barbecued chicken. I don't want you going back to Argentina thinking we have nothing to offer here."

She glanced up to take in Enzo's slouch and sly grin. Was he trying to be sexy or was that just one of his easy talents?

"The last thing I would say," he said, his eyes frozen on her, "is that America. Has. Nothing. To. Offer."

Sofia felt a hot flash rush through her body, but at the same time, she was perturbed that his flattery hit so effectively. "When it comes to cuisine, I mean, my Latin friend," she said sternly.

She finished the corn cobs and started chopping a red bell pepper she'd cored in the sink earlier. She looked up to see if he was still there. He was.

"You could make a girl self-conscious," she said.

Enzo smiled, perhaps in an apology of sorts, and stood up straight. "Do you need some help in here?"

"As long as it'll get you to quit staring, sure," she said. She pointed the knife at the refrigerator. "Do you mind taking the chicken out of the refrigerator and cutting it apart?"

"Love to. Is there another apron?"

Sofia nodded at a tall cabinet in the corner. Enzo pulled out a long white apron, hooked it over his neck and tied the strings in the back. For the next few minutes, they worked side-by-side, humming along with "Thank You for the Music."

Out of the corner of her eye, Sofia saw Enzo glance at her a few times, but she pretended not to notice. She cut up an onion, wiping her nose on the back of her hand, diced up a couple of stalks of celery, and tipped the chopped vegetables into the bowl.

"*Waterloo!*" Enzo yelled. "*The history book on the shelf is always repeating itself,*" he sang, loudly and not particularly well. He put down his knife, wiped his hands on his apron, and reached for Sofia's elbow. He turned her toward him and coaxed her into dropping her knife and joining him in a jitterbug. Rufus got up and left the room, perhaps worried about being stepped on.

Sofia's feet picked up the rhythm, and she sang along with him. "*Waterloo! I was defeated, you won the war. Waterloo! I promise to love you forever more.*" They danced around the island, singing and laughing at themselves.

The song ended, and Enzo raised both arms for a celebratory high-five. Sofia bent over to catch her breath.

"Don't tell me I wore you out!" He laughed. "We are going to have to get you out from behind that desk in Seattle before you can't dance anymore."

THE EARLY EVENING SUN HAD retired early to make way for a weak thunderstorm, but thanks to the broad eaves over the patio, Enzo could still barbecue the chicken outside, collecting only a few drops of rain on his shoulders as he went back and forth from the grill to the kitchen. The light breeze that accompanied the mild storm wafted into the kitchen through the screen door, cooling off the room and scenting it with water-splattered dust of summer.

They sat at the kitchen table, Rufus at their feet, listening to the distant thunder and the patter of rain on the patio stones. Sofia finished her second piece of chicken and licked her fingers for what she figured must have been the 100th time.

"You barbecued this just perfectly," she said, pointing at Enzo with the thigh bone. "Not burned but cooked all the way through."

"It was a great meal. Hats off to you."

"It wasn't nearly as good as your *coq au vin*. And you did half the work."

Enzo grinned and wiped his hands on his napkin before picking up his wine glass.

"We do make a good team, don't we?" he said.

"Yeah, we do." Sofia lifted her glass, and they clinked them together.

"Speaking of teams," Enzo said, "you know there's a tournament next weekend at Wine Valley. Mixed couples. Do you think we could win it?"

Sofia shook her head. "I know you could, but I shot an 85 yesterday. I don't think that's a winning score."

"But you're improving. And I shot a 68. Together, who knows...?"

"And I'm supposed to go back to Seattle on Saturday."

"What's there to go back for? Do you have a date?" Enzo scooped up the last of his vegetables.

"Yes, a date with my job." She pushed her empty plate away and sat back. What would it hurt to stay a little longer?

"Well, on the other hand," she mused, "I do have more vacation coming, and I've done all I can with that marketing campaign for our cider until we can see the latest results."

Enzo watched her, a smile growing on his face as she continued to consider the idea. "And Thomas isn't due back until Wednesday. Maybe ... ."

"Then let's do it!" Enzo exclaimed.

"Can I sleep on it and see how I feel in the morning?"

"No. I think you should decide right now. There aren't many slots left in the roster."

Sofia stood up shaking her head. She gathered their plates and scraped the bones into the trash while she thought it over. "Let me see if I can change my flight."

"Yay!" Enzo clapped excitedly, like they'd already won the tournament, and Rufus barked in agreement.

"Hey, don't get too excited," Sofia said. "It's still possible I'll have to fly home on Saturday. And besides," she picked up and shook a handful of dirty silverware at him, "we still have all these dishes to do."

Two hours later, they were still sitting under the eaves on the patio with Rufus, finishing another bottle of wine and watching the light rain, their conversation having dwindled to a companionable silence.

"I really need to hit the hay," Sofia said.

"What does that mean?" Enzo asked, and Sofia laughed.

"I guess I'm getting so used to your accent that I forget American English isn't your first language. It's an idiom. I guess from when people used to sleep in barns, or on straw mattresses. Something like that. I'm not really sure."

She stood, and Enzo looked up at her with sad eyes. She was tempted to lean down for a good night kiss, but she didn't trust herself. She knew where it could lead.

"Goodnight, Enzo," she said. "I'll call the airline tomorrow morning." Sofia walked to her side of the house, turning off lights as she went. Rufus padded after her and curled up in his usual corner on the foot of the bed. Sofia sat next to him and stroked his head.

"He's an all-right guy, isn't he, buddy?" she asked. Rufus's eyes looked up, but his head was down for the night. "Okay, I'll let you sleep. And I'll keep my opinions to myself."

She changed into her night shirt, brushed her teeth, and crawled in to bed next to him. As she reached up to turn off the bedtable lamp, she noted the time on her phone. It was almost midnight.

"Oh, shoot! she said. Rufus moaned. "I forgot to call Thomas again."

She sat up and texted.

> Sorry. Too late to talk. Got busy. Love you. Talk tomorrow?

As she lay back down, it occurred to her that she'd texted him three times in the last two days, and he'd never responded. Things must be going very well or very badly in Denver, she decided. She'd hear about it soon enough. She pulled the covers up to her neck, closed her eyes, and immediately fell asleep.

Thirteen

Her cellphone's raspy tune woke Sofia before the sun did.

Thomas, she surmised. She leaned over, tipped the phone up to her face, and sat up, surprised. Her mother? Why was she calling so early? She knew Sofia wasn't a particularly early riser.

"Mom," Sofia answered. "Is everything all right?"

"Sofie," her mother replied. "I thought you told me Thomas was going to Denver."

Sofia tossed the covers off and swung her legs over the edge of the bed. Rufus stood up and stretched before jumping down.

"Yes," Sofia said. "He has a marketing meeting there. Until next Wednesday."

"Then why is he sitting here in Sun Valley? Across the restaurant from us? And who is that woman he's sitting next to? She's practically sitting on his lap!"

"I have no idea, Mom. I'll call you back."

Sofia hung up. What would Thomas be doing in Sun Valley? Had they moved the meeting, and he hadn't told her? But how could they afford to fly an entire marketing team up there? The room rates this time of year were astronomical.

She threw a bathrobe over her shoulders, dropped the phone into its pocket, and opened the bedroom door. Rufus padded down the hall and straight to the back door of the kitchen, ready to go out and do his morning business of peeing, sniffing for critters, and securing the perimeter of the yard. Sofia left the door open to let in the fresh air cooled by last night's rain. She glanced out the window to see Enzo's rental car was already gone.

She pulled her phone out of the pocket, planning to call Thomas, but she laid it on the counter instead and drew a carafe of water to make coffee. She wanted to be wide awake before she made that call. Already she sensed the conversation would be difficult. There was no way he brought the marketing team up to Sun Valley. Whatever he was doing up there didn't have anything to do with work.

Her stomach churned with anxiety. She waited for the pot to finish brewing and filled a cup. She sat down at the kitchen table and chose Thomas's phone number from the top of her speed dial list.

It took five rings before he answered. "Sofie?"

"What is going on? You told me you were going to Denver."

"What do you mean?"

"I mean, you're supposed to be in Denver. My mother just called to tell me you were sitting across the restaurant from her in Sun Valley with another woman. Would I be crazy in guessing that might be your new marketing director?"

"Uh … ," Thomas stuttered. "Uh, uh, hold on, I need to get outside. Reception is horrible in here."

Sofia waited, listening for any clues that might tell her where he was and with whom.

She heard the swoosh of a what sounded like a revolving door and then bird chirps that indicated he had made it outside. "What's this about?" he said.

"Are you serious? I just told you I know you're in Sun Valley, and you ask me what this is about?"

A long pause filled the distance between them before Thomas answered. "Sofia, I can explain."

"I think that's a very good idea." Sofia's jaw was so tight she could hardly form words. Her hand was shaking violently, and she punched the speaker and laid the phone on the table.

"I don't know what to say. I ... I ... ," Thomas started.

"Not much of an explanation, Thomas," she retorted. "Just tell me the truth, Thomas. I want the whole truth."

Sofia waited for an answer. Rufus walked back in the kitchen and nuzzled her leg. Time for his breakfast. She reached down and put her hand on his back.

Still Thomas said nothing. Was it silly to ask for the truth when it would be unlikely she'd get it?

"You know, I'm not sure I want to know," she added.

"I'm sorry. The trip to Denver was—"

Sofia interrupted. "There never was a trip to Denver, was there? Thomas. This whole Denver trip was a lie, wasn't it?"

Again, he didn't answer.

"Was it?" she repeated.

"No. Uh. " Thomas hesitated. "You're right. There was no trip to Denver."

Sofia waited for more. Finally, he continued. "I'm sorry, Sofia. We'll have to talk when we get back. We can't do this on the phone."

Sofia let out a whine. "But Sun Valley? Sun Valley is where we met, Thomas. You knew my parents were going to be there. Just how cocky can you get? And who is she?"

Suddenly, Thomas's tongue seemed to find the energy to move. "Sofia," he said, "I'm sorry. I thought maybe I could figure this out if Anna and I got away from Seattle for a few days. I could figure out how I feel about us. And now I know." He paused. "I can't keep leading you on like this. I'm in love with her."

"With Anna and not with me."

"I love you, Sofia. I really do. But you're right. I'm not in love with you." Sofia closed her eyes, hearing the echo of Janet's question: *Are you in love with him?*

"Ever? Were you ever in love with me?" she asked.

"Just not anymore."

Sofia looked up at the ceiling and let the stinging in her eyes deliver a stream of tears. She took a deep breath. Oddly, despite the tears, she felt more relieved than sad.

"You know, maybe this is for the best," she said, trying to hide a sniffle, "getting this over with now. I've known for some time that we weren't ready to get married. And lately, I've started to think maybe we never would be. I love you, Thomas, but I'm not *in love* with you either." She hoped she sounded more certain than she felt.

They let the silence linger for a long time.

"We can talk more when we get back to Seattle," Thomas finally added.

"Right. We can do that." She punched the hang-up button on her phone without saying goodbye. She looked down at Rufus. "And what kind of a guy calls himself Thomas, anyway?"

Her phone's ringtone started again, vibrating the wood table. She looked down and saw it was Enzo. She swiped down to decline the call. "The last thing I need is to talk to you right now." Immediately, it rang again. "Why am I suddenly so damn popular?" Exasperated, she looked at the display again, and this time she answered.

"Hey, have time today to go shopping?" Janet asked cheerfully.

"I … I … Thomas … ." Sofia choked and sobbed.

"I'll be right there," Janet said.

Fifteen minutes later, when Janet arrived at the door, Sofia had changed into sweatpants and had fed Rufus. They returned to the kitchen, and Sofia sat, hugging her knees to her chest. By then, her tears had run their course, leaving her cheeks crusty and leaving Sofia feeling hollowed out.

Janet declined a cup of coffee. She reached into a cabinet and pulled out the vodka. She poured a glass and set it in front of Sofia.

"What's this?" Sofia frowned.

"It's vodka."

"I only drink wine, and it's still morning."

Janet nodded emphatically. "Right. But wine is for happy times. And lots of people drink vodka for breakfast. Screwdrivers. Bloody Marys." She turned, pulled out another glass, and poured some for herself.

Sofia lifted the glass and inspected it. "I don't see any juice here."

"Think of it as a screwdriver with a little less orange juice and a little more vodka."

"I can't believe you're making jokes when I just broke up with my fiancé"

Janet snorted. "Look, I feel bad for you. But first, he's not technically your fiancé, is he? I see no ring. And I don't know if it's really a break-up if you were never getting married in the first place. And third, I never liked the guy."

"Come on Janet. A little sympathy here. I loved him. Once upon a time, like yesterday, I thought we'd have a future together."

Janet sat down next to her and sipped her vodka, looking thoughtful. "I can't figure out how he hid this Anna person from you. They must have been seeing each other a lot."

Sofia lifted the glass to her lips and wet them. She put it back down. "I didn't see anything. Maybe I was working too hard. Maybe I didn't want to see anything."

She put the glass to her lips again and took a long sip. The vodka burned her throat and she coughed.

"Hey, shouldn't you be at work?" she asked when she could talk again.

"This is more important," Janet said. "It's not like this is the busy season. All the farmers are getting ready for harvest, not thinking about loans right now. None of the vintners worries about finances until after the crush. Besides, I called you to see about shopping, remember?"

Sofia sniffed sarcastically. "Somehow, that slipped my mind." She took another sip of vodka. It still burned, but less so. "Thanks for coming over. I know there's nothing you can do, but it helps to talk with someone."

"I wish I could do something more. Like murder Thomas. Has he ever cheated on you before?"

"Not that I know of."

"How about lying? Has he lied to you?"

Sofia considered the question. "Yes. A few times. But it was silly stuff. How many martinis he had on the way home from work ... that sort of thing."

"Wow, this kind of betrayal has to be hard."

Sofia nodded. She raked her fingers through her hair, pushing her bangs straight back. Then she shook her head. "Maybe it's not as hard as it should be. I think I was already starting to pull away. I could feel he was. But I still didn't see this coming. You should have seen our anniversary dinner. He ordered Dom Perignon!"

Janet snorted again. "He struck me as that kind of guy. Big on the show. And big on himself."

"Maybe," Sofia muttered. She wasn't sure she agreed.

"Maybe what you saw was just how serious he was about his career. He's going to go somewhere. It takes that kind of commitment if you're going to succeed."

"Relationships take commitment too, you know."

"Don't lecture me, Janet. I'm not the one who's in Sun Valley with my new marketing assistant," Sofia said, tipping up the glass and draining the vodka. "Heck, I don't even have an assistant."

Janet finished her vodka and the two sat in silence for a couple of minutes.

"It may take a while before I put myself out there again," Sofia said. "I need to focus on my career. Find a way back into the wine business. You know," she paused, "I haven't dated anyone but Thomas since I finished college and started my job. I haven't even looked at another guy in three years."

Janet smirked. "Until Enzo."

Sofia slapped Janet's arm. "What are you saying? I am not 'looking' at Enzo. He's staying here because Michael invited him."

"Oh, come on. You told me the other night he was growing on you. Didn't you almost kiss?"

Sofia pouted. "I can't believe you are bringing that up now. Your timing sucks, my friend." She stood up and pulled the carafe from the coffee pot and poured herself another cup. The last thing she needed to add to this impending depression was more alcohol.

Janet nodded and twisted her lips. "I'm sorry. I don't know what I'm saying. I guess I'd really like to see you with someone who makes you happy."

Fourteen

With every swing of the club, Sofia felt better.

Out on the driving range, nearly finished hitting two hundred practice balls, Sofia considered how the almost violent act of smashing the clubhead against defenseless little white balls over and over again enlisted muscle, sinew, and bone in the service of clearing the mind. With something like seventy things to remember in every one-second swing—among them: keep the head behind the ball, keep the left arm straight, maintain the triangle formation of arms and chest, start the swing with the hips not the arms, keep the head level, maintain the spine angle, finish with 90 percent of your weight on your front foot, turn the hands over beginning at impact—there wasn't a lot of brain power left to noodle one's angst. It was a bit like a deep, dreamless sleep. With her conscious mind focusing on the swing, her subconscious could work out her problems. Or not.

With six balls left, Sofia decided to forget all seventy

things and just focus on generating as much brutal power as possible. She tried to imagine the ball as Anna's face, but realized she had no idea what the woman looked like. "I guess Thomas's face will have to suffice," she muttered.

Apparently, the work she'd put in on her technique with the first 194 balls had done its trick. Every one of the last six shots went straight down the middle and farther than she'd ever hit a ball with a driver in her life. "Huh!" she huffed, breathless from the effort, watching the last ball sail far past the 200-yard marker. "Maybe I just need to swing harder."

She looked back at the pile of clubs she'd left lying on the ground next to her bag and saw Enzo standing behind her, smiling.

"How long have you been standing there?" she asked. "You should have warned me."

"Looked like you're working on more than your golf swing," he said. "I didn't want to disturb the process."

"How—?"

"Janet told me. She called me and told me what happened."

"That wasn't for her—"

"She was only worried about you. She thought maybe I should come and check on you. It's great to have good friends like that."

Sofia pursed her lips. It was hard to argue with any of what he said. It probably would help not to be alone for the next day or so. A little sympathy and camaraderie could mend a lot of hurt.

"Look, I'm sorry. I don't know this guy Thomas, but I can't imagine he found anyone as great as you."

Sofia looked off into the distance and tried not to tear up. It wasn't as if she didn't know breaking up with Thomas was the right thing to happen. It was something else: the experience of failing, the end of a shared history, the loss of a friend. It all made her sad.

"Maybe I'm really not so great."

"I think you are." Enzo stepped toward her and offered her his arms. She accepted. His hug was solid and comforting without a hint of erotic intent. She rested her head on his shoulder for a good minute. She couldn't remember ever receiving an embrace as consoling and calming as this.

Enzo gently pushed her away. "Hey, come on. Let's get out of here and go for a walk."

Sofia wiped the tears from her cheeks with the back of her golf glove and bent down to pick up a club. Enzo helped her put them away, and then he picked the heavy bag and led the way back up to the parking lot. She flipped open the trunk of her car, and he tossed the bag in.

"I'll meet you at your house," he said. "We should stop there first so we can take Rufus with us."

Mention of Rufus made her smile for the first time that day.

RUFUS HAD GONE CRAZY AS soon as he realized he was going to get to ride in a car, and he ran circles around it until Sofia got the door open so he could jump in. Enzo drove to Lion's Park on the east side of town with Rufus hanging his head out the backseat window.

Enzo parked and hooked Rufus on a retractable leash, and the three of them headed downstream along the canal.

They watched Rufus sniff and mark and sniff and mark with happy abandon, saying nothing to each other, for a quarter mile. Sofia breathed deeply, imagining she was expelling any negative vapors that had built up since the call from her mother that morning.

Finally, Enzo spoke quietly. "I tried to call you to tell you we got the last spot in the tournament on Saturday. Actually, someone cancelled, or we wouldn't—"

Sofia interrupted. "I don't think I can do it."

Enzo nodded. He didn't argue. He looked up at the

tops of the trees and at the wetlands beside the trail. "It is really beautiful here. I can see why people never leave," he said.

Sofia let out a little laugh. "Oh, lots of people leave. And you wouldn't say that in January in the middle of a blizzard that blows in all the way from the Cascades. It's not so beautiful then."

"I suppose," he said. "But if it weren't for winter, the vines would get no rest."

Sofia looked over at him, humored. "Are you always thinking about vines? About grapes and wine? What is it about wine that produces that kind of devotion?"

"I don't know." He paused and rubbed his chin. "Maybe it's the way the vines have to suffer in order to produce the sweetest fruit. The way grow in rocky, dry soil, and survive freezing winters."

They walked a few more feet before he continued. "Maybe it teaches us something about life ... that it's not the easy path that makes us strong."

That made Sofia chuckle. She flashed him a sardonic look. "If I were a suspicious kind of woman, I'd think you've used that line before."

Enzo looked back at her, grinning. "What makes you think I haven't?"

"And how has it worked in the past?" she asked.

Enzo looked down the path ahead and shook his head. "A little better than it did just now."

They walked a little farther in silence. A light breeze made the sunlight flicker through the trees onto the trail. Little critters scampered deep in the leaves and the grass beside them, and Rufus stopped them now and then to stick his nose into the ground cover. A squirrel raced across the road in front of them, and Rufus pulled hard on the leash. Enzo stopped him with the leash brake and gently pulled him back.

"You're good with him," Sofia remarked.

"Yeah, well, I've had dogs forever."

A few steps later he added, "Mine is a simple life, Sofia. Wine, golf, and dogs. Now you know everything there is to know about me."

"Hmm. No girlfriends? No wives? No concubines?"

Enzo looked puzzled. "Concubines? I don't think I know that word."

"Mistresses," Sofia said.

He laughed. "Ah! No. No mistresses. But, to tell you the truth, I was dating a woman for a year or so." He paused, and his face looked like he was trying to figure out how to explain.

"It's part of the reason I'm here," he said finally. "To get away."

Sofia frowned and then worked to rid it from her face. "You never said anything about her."

"Not much to say." But then he elaborated anyway. "Christina. Christina Montoya. I'm afraid she is more interested in my ... no, let me rephrase that. She is more interested in our winery than in me."

"Why do you say that?"

"Her family and mine have been competing for years over whose vineyards make the best wines. She has been estranged from her father, and I think she's trying to get even with him."

"By dating you?"

Enzo nodded. "Yes. She makes all the right moves, says all the right things in public. But in private, she closes off. It's like she's only with me to get her father's attention." He looked at Sofia with a crooked smile that deepened his dimples. "Perhaps I'm not handsome enough?"

Sofia blushed. "Ummm. Something tells me that's not it."

Enzo mugged a funny face.

"Why? Do you think I'm handsome?"

Now Sofia laughed fully for the first time that day. "You are begging for a compliment?"

"Yes, I am," Enzo said and echoed her laugh.

They walked a little farther and Sofia spoke again.

"But you felt more for her than she did for you. Is that the problem?"

"It was. But this time away … it's been good for me. It's helped me put those feelings aside finally. I don't miss her like I once thought I would. What I thought was love was only fear at losing her. When I go back, it will be over."

Out of the corner of her eye, Sofia saw him look over at her meaningfully, as if he were waiting for her to approve. She looked down at Rufus and avoided his eyes.

"So, you haven't talked to her since you got here?" she asked.

"I've been busy."

"Not that busy." Sofia bumped into him playfully, but Enzo's expression didn't change. They kept walking.

"You know, I don't miss Thomas either," Sofia said. "I realized that the second day I was here. Actually, it's been good to be away from him. Like freeing. But I thought I'd feel different after a week apart. Now, I do, but not in the way I thought."

Enzo said nothing.

"And," she added, "by the way, Rufus doesn't like him."

"Well, that should have been a deal breaker." They laughed together. "Why don't you tell me about your life in Seattle," he continued. "I've always wanted to visit there."

Enzo was sitting out on the patio, absent-mindedly scratching Rufus's head. Sofia watched him for a minute through the glass door before sliding it open with her foot, a bottle of wine in one hand and a bowl of olives in the other. Enzo glanced up, looking like he was having trouble leaving his daydream, and smiled.

"Another beautiful sunset," he said. "Do you ever get tired of them?"

Sofia's eyes followed his eyes out over the vineyard. "No," she answered. "Never." She paused, frozen by the view. "We get beautiful sunsets over the water in Seattle, too. But only about two months of the year. Rest of the time, it's too cloudy to see them."

She shook herself away from her gaze and put the olives and wine on the table.

"Thanks. Two of my favorite things—wine and olives," he said. "You know what my third favorite is?"

Sofia's heart jumped. "No, what?" she whispered.

"Rufus." Enzo bent down to let the big dog smother his face with his big tongue.

Sofia laughed. "Why was I thinking ... ?"

"Thinking what?"

"Never mind." Embarrassed, Sofia turned to grab two wine glasses from the cabinet under the eaves. "By the way," she said over her shoulder. "I changed my flight so we can play on Saturday. I'm staying another week."

Enzo wound himself out of his seat and stood with his arms open and the biggest grin Sofia had seen yet. "The best news ever!" he exclaimed. "I thought you would, so I didn't cancel our slot in the tournament." Sofia stepped into his big hug, but immediately, a jealous Rufus stood up and squeezed between them.

Sofia laughed and stepped away from man and beast and reached for a corkscrew in the cabinet drawer. She handed it to Enzo. "You open the bottle. We have to plan our tournament strategy."

Fifteen

THE TOURNAMENT'S SEVENTY-TWO GOLFERS MINGLED in the pink light of dawn, spreading over the putting green and out to the driving range. They milled around the golf carts lined up for the shotgun start, studying the tournament rules and the tournament scorecards clipped to the steering wheels.

Sofia looked anxiously for Enzo's rental car as she chatted with old friends from her high school golf team and older golfers who played with her parents. Enzo wasn't late yet, but there wasn't much time left for him to warm up or practice putting.

Finally, she saw him pull up to the club drop, leave his bag on the stand, and then maneuver into one of the last parking spots left. She trotted out to meet him as he walked back toward her and toward the clubhouse.

"You don't have much time. Going to warm up a bit?" she asked a few yards before reaching him.

"I overslept," he said as he approached with a sheepish grin. "I think all those late nights on the patio are starting to take a toll."

"What? Do you go to bed at sundown in Argentina?"

"You probably think that's funny, but yes," he said, matching her stride back to the sign-in tent and pulling her in for a sideways hug. "If you've hit balls already, I'll just putt a few. Get the feel for the greens."

They reached the tent, and Enzo ducked inside to check in. When he re-emerged, Sofia grabbed his arm.

"I have some people you should meet," she said. She led him to a knot of men and women, all about their age, chatting, laughing and exchanging bets over the coming contest.

"Hey, guys," she shouted. They opened their circle for her and Enzo, and she introduced him.

"Another Argentinian, huh?" said Donna, a woman Sofia had known forever but never much liked, setting several others to laughing. Sofia punched her in the arm.

"I can see what you see in them, though," Donna responded, winking and rubbing her arm as if Sofia's jab had really hurt.

"Enzo's here for a couple of weeks, studying wine marketing," Sofia explained. "He used to play professionally back home."

A few impressed murmurs replaced the giggles, and a couple of the men stepped up to shake Enzo's hand. "Played here before?" asked one, and Sofia left Enzo to tell his own stories while she made a final trip to the clubhouse restroom.

SOFIA AND ENZO PULLED UP to their first tee of the tournament and jumped out to greet the other two of their four-some. Betsy and Carl Werther were of an age somewhere between Sofia and her parents, and although she had known them for years, she had never played with them.

"I heard you were back in town," Betsy said to Sofia, giving her a quick, platonic hug. "Are you staying or going back to Seattle?"

"Going back," Sofia said, and stepped back to let Enzo introduce himself to the couple. Why, she wondered, did everyone think she might come back to town? Was that a thing these days? Sofia had seen that the wine business—both production and tourism—was booming, but it was it really bringing people back? Or maybe people who stayed just liked to think they knew a good thing before she did, and that she might just now be catching on.

Sofia was reluctant to go back to Seattle. But was it the vineyards and the wine business? Or was it simply her job? She liked Walla Walla and was proud of her family history there, but she still didn't feel the draw that everyone seemed to be alluding to. Maybe it had been Thomas that kept her in Seattle, and now there was no more Thomas, she could decide what she wanted her future to look like.

Carl stepped up to the tee box and took a couple of easy practice swings like a man who played golf regularly. No hitches, no shyness on the first tee like Sofia remembered feeling when she first started playing golf.

Whack! The ball few down the middle of the fairway about two hundred yards—nothing an amateur golfer would be ashamed of.

"Nice shot, man. Keep them in the middle like that and you'll never get in trouble," Enzo commented as he walked up to place his tee in the ground. He stepped back, picked his target, and as usual, stepped up and teed off without a practice swing. The ball sailed well past the one-fifty-yard mark, landing at about 255 yards, only eighty yards shy of the green.

Sofia watched Carl's face. At first, he smiled, and then as he followed the ball, his eyes widened, and his jaw dropped.

"Well, I guess we know who the real competition is going to be today!" he said. He clapped Enzo on the back as they headed back to the carts.

At the forward tees, Sofia hit a great drive as well, nearly reaching Enzo's thanks to the sixty-yard advantage the tee box gave her, and Betsy kept hers in the fairway. Their round was started.

The tournament was set up as a shamble, which allowed each couple to play their second shots from where their best tee-shot landed. With Enzo's long drives and Sofia's short-game skills kicking in, she and Enzo penciled in a few birdies the first nine holes. Betsy and Carl took the stiff competition well.

"I always play better when I play with good golfers," Betsy commented after she putted in for a birdie on the ninth hole.

Sofia thought they couldn't have picked another couple that would have been as pleasant to play with.

At the turn, Enzo and Sofia grabbed a couple of beers and relieved themselves in the clubhouse restrooms. As they waited in the shade of their golf cart for Betsy and Carl to catch up to them on the tenth tee box, Sofia gazed out at the purple hills far to the west and sighed deeply.

"What was that for?" Enzo asked.

"Just thinking I can't remember a better day in my entire life," she said, still staring at the view.

Enzo tapped her on the shoulder, and she turned to face him. He smiled and leaned forward, and she met his lips half-way. The kiss was brief, cut short by the arrival of their playing partners. But it set Sofia's head swimming, and she hesitated before stepping out of the cart.

"I didn't realize you two were—" Betsy started to tease as the men stepped up to their tee box.

Sofia cut her off. "We're not. I mean we're not what that probably looked like."

She felt her face heat up. She wished she didn't blush so easily.

"Well, I don't know why you're not," Betsy said. "Seems like a pretty nice match to me."

As the men waited for the group ahead to clear the fairway, Sofia remembered that she and Julio had first kissed on this golf course too—and how their relationship had ended here, with the policemen leading two naked teenagers back to where they'd left their clothes, and then escorting them back to Sofia's parents. It was time, she decided, to quit thinking of it as a nightmare. It wasn't. It was fun and funny and, yes, in the end embarrassing, but the love and the reckless abandon were special. Had she ever captured that since?

On the tough tenth hole, Enzo chipped in for an eagle, and Sofia walked over and pulled his face down to hers and gave him a noisy smack on the lips.

"Bravo, partner," she whispered. He flashed his big grin and pulled her to him. This time, their kiss was long and passionate, and Sofia backed away from it out of breath, her heart pounding. They walked back to the cart with Enzo's arm over her shoulder and hers around his waist.

"Liar," Betsy said.

Although she was tempted to embrace Enzo every time one of their putts dropped, Sofia kept her distance for the next few holes, and rewarded his great shots with only a smile. Displays of affection on the golf course were disrespectful to both the playing partners and the game, and Enzo apparently believed that as well.

As the last ball fell into the final hole, though, they were ready to celebrate. They hopped toward each other for an energetic high-five, but their hands missed. Doubled over laughing, Sofia felt Enzo's arm reach over her back, and she rose for another passionate kiss. She didn't want it to end, and for a long time, it didn't. Betsy and Carl drove back to the clubhouse, leaving them alone on the green.

Sixteen

Sofia breathed deeply to tamp down her emotions as the crowd of golfers gathered on the patio for a late lunch and the announcement of the day's winners. She had a pretty good feeling that their gross score, two under par, might hold up as the best of the day. But that wasn't what was making her smile.

They sat at a table with their day's partners, Carl and Betsy, as players usually do at couple's tournaments, and talked over their good shots and bad shots before they forgot them. They toasted birdies and laughed about the shanks that led to bogies. The hamburger and steak fries were fine, but Sofia had a hard time focusing on her food. She kept glancing at Enzo and seeing a completely different man than she had met less than a week ago. And he looked back at her in a way she had never anticipated days before. As he talked to Carl or Betsy, she studied his expressions, and when she spoke, he watched as if seeking hidden meanings in her face. She could hardly wait for the party to break up so they could start their evening on the patio over the vineyard.

"Hello, hello. Can you hear me?" John, the golf pro, stepped up to the edge of the patio just above the drop-off to the fairway below, microphone in hand. The speaker beside him squawked, and he adjusted the dial.

"Before we hand out the trophies to today's winners, I want to thank you all for coming out and enduring this horrible weather." He pointed out at the sunny fairway, and the golfers laughed politely.

"And thanks to our staff for putting on an absolutely perfect tournament. Let's give them a hand."

Sofia joined the others, cheering and clapping for the staff who stood across the patio from John, their backs leaning up against the clubhouse.

"And, now, without further blabbing from me, I'd like to present our winners." The patio fell silent. "In third place, with a net score of 146, Betsy and Carl Werther."

Sofia and Enzo stood and clapped wildly as their playing partners got up and walked up to John. He handed them each a small trophy of a golfer in a finishing pose engraved with the tournament name and date. A photographer stepped up and took their picture standing next to John. They returned to the table, smiling proudly.

"And in second place, with a net score of 144, a perfect par, Teresa and Blake Thompson."

A couple seated across the patio got up and went through the same routine. Once they returned toward their seats, John continued.

"And in first place, with an amazing, yet official and attested, combined gross score of 134, a 128 net, are our own Sofia Michaelis and her new partner, Enzo Benedetti!"

New partner? Sofia tried that on for size in her mind. Could Enzo be her new partner?

She blushed as the golfers stood, clapped, and whooped for her and Enzo. Enzo took her hand, and they walked up to John.

"And they might be the best-looking couple out here today too," John added, making Sofia's face grow even hotter. Enzo accepted the big trophy and turned to let Sofia help him hold it up high. The photographer stepped forward and snapped a picture.

It didn't surprise Sofia when Enzo turned and put his free hand on the back of her head. She leaned forward, eyes closed for a celebratory kiss.

Just as their lips met, a clubhouse door banged open, and everyone turned to see a diminutive, attractive blonde stumble out in stilettos, a short, tight skirt, and the biggest hairdo Sofia had ever seen in her life.

"Enzo!" the woman shouted. "I look all over for you! I should know you be on the golf course."

The woman strutted across the patio to Enzo as Sofia stepped back. Just before she reached them, the woman seemed to suddenly spy Sofia. Briefly, she paused, but then she approached Enzo, pulled his face down to hers, and kissed him passionately.

The photographer, apparently afraid to miss Walla Walla's photographic opportunity of the century, squeezed off a few quick shots of their lips smashed together.

Sofia studied Enzo's face as it was bent to the woman's. Rather than closing his eyes, he strained to look over at Sofia. All the effort in the kiss was the woman's, but he didn't pull away. Sofia stood back, now holding the trophy alone.

"*Felicitaciones, mi cariño. Ganaste otra vez?*" the woman chirped as she finally stopped her smooch. She grabbed Enzo's hand, pointed at the trophy, and looked at Sofia with a patronizing smile. The woman poked her hand toward Sofia to shake.

"Hello. I'm Christina, Enzo's girlfriend from Mendoza.

It looks like you are to be congratulated also?"

Sofia accepted Christina's limp clasp and quickly let go. The other golfers, who at first seemed intrigued by the scene, had already turned away and resumed their conversations. John, however, watched the strange trio, frowning.

Christina stood between Enzo and Sofia, looking back and forth. "You play together today? You must be very good, Sofia. He never play with me. I don't do golfing, really, you know."

"No, I didn't know. I'd never guess." Sofia didn't try to withhold the sarcasm from her voice.

Christina smiled, apparently not recognizing the tone, and turned to grab Enzo's hands. "Can we go now? I'm starving. And I want you show me around. This is so quaint little place. But is Walla Walla a real name?"

Sofia started to walk back to their table, but Enzo reached out for her arm.

"Sofia, wait! I will give you a ride home," he pleaded.

Sofia pulled her arm free. "No, I drove myself, remember? You slept in. And, in retrospect," she nodded at Christina, "it appears to have been well-timed."

She took a step away. "And everyone here knows me, so I'm sure they'll want to thank me for giving them another embarrassing story about Sofia Michealis and her Argentinian to remember."

She turned back to Christina. "It was wonderful to meet you, Christina. I hope you enjoy your stay at my family's home." She looked to Enzo. "I'll be out of there before you get back from your dinner and tour of the city."

"But your flight isn't until next week," he said.

"I think I'll stay with Janet for a couple of days," Sofia answered, forcing a benevolent smile. "We haven't had much of a chance to see each other." She held out her hand to Enzo. "Goodbye, Enzo. Safe travels home."

Sofia's hands were sweating, and her heart pounded

as she snuck back to the table with Carl and Betsy. She tried to ignore Betsy's expression—a mix of sympathy and mortification—and put on a big, happy smile. She held up the trophy victoriously, and let Betsy take a picture of her standing with it.

Sofia sat down, and they stumbled into a jumbled conversation that went nowhere. Sofia watched Enzo and Christina walk around the patio toward the parking lot. Enzo glanced back at her, and she looked away.

Seventeen

Sofia placed the trophy she and Enzo won on the mantle over the big stone fireplace in the living room of her parents' home. She stepped back and looked. It wasn't quite centered. She adjusted it and stepped back again. A tear dropped onto the wood floor at her feet. She wiped angrily at her eyes with the back of her hand and swore.

She stood and stared at the tall golfer atop the award. His arms were extended high above his back and his weight was solidly balanced on his front foot. How many times in a round, she wondered, did she execute a perfect finish like that? How many times did Enzo? She grimaced. He completed every swing as if it were going to be memorialized in just such a statue as the one atop the trophy.

Yes, he was perfect. Perfect in most ways, anyway. Perhaps not when it came to taking control of his love life. If he really didn't love Christina, as he said, he should have convinced her of that long before she flew all the way to this backwater town in southeastern Washington to ruin Sofia's otherwise perfect day.

She turned and walked out to the patio through the open door and stared at the late afternoon light reflecting off the fluttering grape leaves below. Rufus lifted his head off his paws, yawned, and put it back down. He was lucky. He got to stay there for the rest of his life. She was going back to Seattle the next morning. Who knew when she'd get back to these glorious afternoons?

She stood with her hands on her hips and flashed back to the evenings she'd spent out there with Enzo. How much time she'd spent resisting her attraction to him! For what? For Thomas? Thomas who never kissed her the way Enzo had that afternoon. Twice. And what a brutal tease those kisses had been. He'd be back in Argentina with Christina in no time, and Sofia would be back in Seattle, loveless and alone, working at a job she didn't like in an industry she didn't respect.

"Just how sorry can I feel for myself?" she asked aloud. "Get your life together, Sofia. It's no one's fault but your own that you have nothing to go back for." Seattle had one of the country's hottest job markets. Her marketing experience was valuable across industries; she just had to decide what she wanted. And only four other cities in the country had a higher percentage of young adults living solo. There were plenty of bachelors there. She just had to put some effort into finding one. If she wanted to. Now she wasn't sure. Maybe the best antidote to the Thomas and Enzo fiascos was a very long time alone.

After a minute, Sofia shook off her self-pity and her memories, and tossed her car keys in her hand. She walked back through the house, followed by Rufus, grabbed her rollerbag, and pulled it out to the car. Rufus lay down on the sidewalk with his head on his paws again and whined a little. Sofia threw her bag in the trunk on top of her golf clubs and turned to take a last look at the house.

"Goodbye, Rufus," she said. "Your buddy Enzo will be back shortly. Bite his girlfriend for me."

She lowered herself into the driver's seat. As she turned the corner onto the highway, she saw Enzo's car approaching, signaling its turn onto the driveway. She stared straight ahead. If he recognized her, if he waved, she didn't see it.

SOFIA'S HEAD DROOPED OVER HER coffee cup. Despite Janet's attempt to make her comfortable, Sofia hadn't slept much. And although her friend had made pancakes and bacon—their favorite breakfast way back when they played on the golf team together—Sofia couldn't eat.

"I didn't know how I felt about him until it was too late," she muttered, just barely loud enough for Janet to hear. "Honestly, just 10 minutes before she showed up, we were celebrating and talking about me coming to visit him in Argentina. Then, she struts in. And I just stood there like a jilted lover at the altar with the whole town staring at me. Me making a fool of myself with another Argentinian. Geez, I'm pathetic."

"But what did he say?" Janet asked, tearing pieces of bacon off a slice by hand and chewing them one-by-one. "Was he happy to see her?"

"I don't know. He let her kiss him. Right there in front of everyone. Right after everyone saw him kiss me."

Janet shook her head. "Ugh, how embarrassing! So, she stayed with him? Up at your house? That just stinks!"

"That's why I had to get out of there. And why I have to get out of here today." She snorted derisively. "I'll bet she doesn't even like dogs."

Sofia looked up at Janet. "Do you know she doesn't play golf?"

Janet's mouth formed a fine line. There wasn't much she could say that would help, and it looked like she was trying not to say anything that would make matters worse.

Slowly, Sofia sipped her coffee, until it was finally too cold to drink. She pushed it away.

"I guess I'd better go. My flight leaves in an hour." The two women stood up, and Janet gave her a hug.

"You'll be okay alone in Seattle? Want me to come and stay for a few days?" Janet asked.

"No. I think I need some time alone to figure things out. Maybe I'll quit my job and come back here eventually. Turns out Rufus is apparently the love of my life."

"I'd love to have you come back. But don't rush into anything. You've been through a lot the past couple of days. No rash decisions. Okay?"

Sofia nodded. "I won't. I promise."

She grabbed her rollerbag's handle and started to the door. Janet passed her and held it open. She kissed Sofia on the cheek as she stepped out.

Sofia rolled her bag down the front steps, and as she reached the sidewalk, she looked up and stopped.

Enzo was leaning against his car at the curb, arms crossed over his chest. He straightened up, dropped his arms, and walked toward her. He placed his hands on her shoulders.

"You can't leave," he said. His eyes were pleading. "I can't let you leave. Not without me."

"What do you mean?" Sofia demanded. She looked around him for Christina. "Where is she?"

"She's gone. Back to Argentina. I just took her to the airport."

"But you two looked so … ."

"Miserable?" Enzo finished for her. "Or did I just look like I didn't know my head from my tail?"

Sofia looked away from his face and shook his hands off her shoulders. "Why did she come?"

"I was ignoring her texts. She says she was worried

about me. Turns out, she had reason to be. I had fallen in love with someone else."

Sofia shook her head and turned her back to him.

"I'm sorry, Sofia," Enzo said, talking over her shoulder. "Even before I left Mendoza, I knew that it was over with her. But when she showed up like that yesterday, I didn't want to embarrass you by making a scene in front of all of those people."

Sofia stood with her arms crossed over her chest. He walked around to face her.

"I remembered what you said about Julio humiliating you in front of the entire town. I wanted to get out of there as quickly as possible. I needed to go somewhere else to tell Christina that we were over. I couldn't do it there in front of everyone."

Sofia was looking away from him.

"Sofia?" He bent to look at her.

Sofia closed her eyes for a moment, and then looked up at the trees, sunlight winking through as a light breeze rustled the leaves.

"You are telling me it's over between you?" she asked.

"Yes. I knew it a week ago. Sofia, I knew it the minute I met you."

She looked into his face. "But you have to go back to Argentina. Sooner or later, you'll get back with her. She'll make sure you do."

"Not if you come with me."

Sofia frowned. "Come with you? What are you talking about? My home is in Seattle. I work there. My life is there."

Enzo nodded and reached for a hand. Reluctantly, she allowed him to hold it.

"Look," he said, "you're not crazy about your job. You want to get back to working with wine. Lots of wineries in Argentina—not just mine—need help with marketing. I think you should come down to visit your brother. Maybe you'll decide to stay. Maybe you'll let me love you."

The word "love" surprised and muted her. She caught her breath and thought for a minute. She was crazy to believe him. She would be crazy to quit her job and fly to another hemisphere on the chance that she'd found the love of her life in Enzo. That he could make room in his life for her.

She tried to stay calm, but she couldn't stop the smile working its way across her lips. Her heart was pounding, telling her what she wanted. Enzo. And it sounded like he wanted her. Finally, she looked up at him. "Are you serious?"

"I want you. I won't leave without you."

Sofia held his eyes as he stepped close.

"Sofie. I love you." He put a finger under her chin and lifted her face toward his. He kissed her lightly.

Sofia closed her eyes and let out a sob. Could she trust this? Could she believe he loved her?

Could she not?

"I love you too," she said. She put her arms over his shoulders and pulled him in.

Eighteen

Sofia burst through the door onto Enzo's patio, where he sat with his parents, having a late afternoon cocktail.

"Sorry I'm late," she said, nodding at the elders.

Enzo stood up and grabbed Sofia's hand. "*Lo siento*," he said to his parents. "We need to talk in private."

He led her at a trot down between the vineyard rows as the sun set in the west behind huge, snow-capped mountain peaks. The big dog, Vino, jogged ahead of them, stopping every few yards to sniff the wake of some critter that had passed through before.

Once they were out of earshot of the patio, Enzo slowed down. "Now, I can't wait any longer. Tell me what happened!"

"I didn't think I had a chance." Sofia paused to catch her breath. "Back in Walla Walla they said I didn't know enough people to do marketing for a wine region. But here, they said with your help and my brother's, I can make all the connections I need. I figured, why not? So, I said yes. I took the job. I start next week."

"So, you will stay here in Mendoza?"

"Si, Señor." She grinned. "I am going to stay here as long as you want me."

"That will be forever!" He stopped and picked Sofia up with his arms around her waist and twirled around. Vino loped back to them and barked. Enzo let Sofia down and kissed her softly. He took her hand, and they continued walking between the vines.

"I don't think I ever realized how beautiful dusk is until I spent those evenings on your patio with Rufus," he said, looking out over the vines toward the setting sun.

"And with me?" she asked.

Enzo smiled mischievously. "Oh, were you there too?"

Sofia laughed, and reached down to scratch an ear of the big dog walking beside her. "Well, I never knew I could love another dog as much as I love Rufus." She joined Enzo's gaze at the horizon. "And I never knew I would find a place I loved as much I loved that patio back home," she whispered. "But this is just as beautiful."

Enzo stopped again and turned her to face him. "Welcome to your new home, my love."

Their kiss lasted long after the sun finally dipped behind the mountains and the vineyard grew dark.

Author's Note

I started writing these novellas as screenplays about a month into the Covid-19 quarantine. I had passed the time that first month watching Hallmark Channel movies—something I had never done before. I found the films calming and mind-numbing in a good way. The formula was easy enough to parse, and Hallmark's guidelines are laid out clearly on its website: no violence and no sex. From watching, it was clear that swearing, religion, and politics were off-limits as well. Once I finished the screenplays, I turned them into these novellas. I imagine the readers most likely to enjoy this book will be those who enjoy Hallmark's romantic films. But even if you've never watched one in your life, I hope you find these stories calming and fun to read. Now that you've enjoyed Love Between the Vines, try the other two: Everyone Loves Zelda and Love on the Links.

About the Author

MARJORIE PINKERTON MILLER* IS THE romance pen name for Marj Charlier, author of nine contemporary and historical novels, two romance novels, and three romance novellas. Her first historical novel, *The Rebel Nun*, was published by Blackstone Publishing and won first-place prizes for historical fiction and overall fiction in the 2023 Colorado Independent Book Publishers Association EVVY awards. A former *Wall Street Journal* reporter, she holds degrees in journalism from Iowa State University and the University of Wisconsin-Madison, and an MBA from Regis University. She lives and works in Colorado Springs, CO, with her husband, the journalist Ben Miller.

*Pinkerton was the author's paternal grandmother's maiden name, and Miller was her mother's maiden name. Marjorie is her given name.

www.ingramcontent.com/pod-product-compliance
Lightning Source LLC
Chambersburg PA
CBHW021558310726
48972CB00003B/849